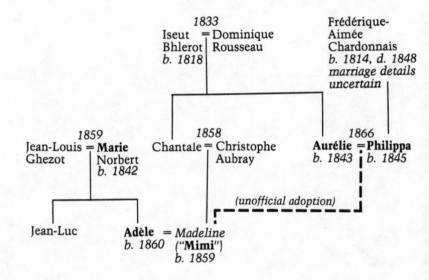

**Boldface** indicates major characters in this book.

Marriage symbol ( = ) is used to indicate all long-term relationships

# Légende

### The story of Philippa and Aurelie

### by Jeannine Allard

Boston: Alyson Publications, Inc.

This is a paperback original from Alyson Publications, Inc., PO Box
2783, Boston, MA  02208. Distributed in England by Gay Men's
Press, PO Box 247, London, N15 6RW.

First edition, May 1984        5   4   3   2   1

ISBN 0 932870 50 3

*To Julie,*
*who helped me find the dreams;*

*To Marcia,*
*who gave me the courage to take them seriously;*

*and to Richard,*
*who never stops challenging them —*
*and me — to grow.*

# Author's Note

Sometime early on last century, two women living on the coast of France loved each other. They didn't know how to do this and survive, so one of them posed as a man, and they were married in the village church.

The one who pretended to be a man was lost at sea, as were so many sailors before technology caught up with navigation; and the other, unable to face life alone, killed herself. A statue was erected along the coast in their honor, symbolizing all of those who have been lost, and have lost those that they love, to the sea.

Later, the identity of the sailor was discovered. Enraged that they had been duped for so many years, the angry and frightened townspeople pushed the statue off into the sea.

I don't know how much, if any, of this story is true. I heard two variations of it: one in Brittany, sitting up late in a farm kitchen drinking cider and sharing stories, and another in Paris — the latter claimed that it happend in Normandy, not Brittany, and that there was also a child involved.

It might be true; or it might well be one of those legends that spring up from time to time and fascinate the imagination of those who are open to them. But, true or not, it's a good story: a story of hope, and love, and strength. The village of Saint-Pol-des-Fougères does not exist; nor do the characters of Philippa and Aurélie and the others represent real people, either living or dead. I chose Brittany because it is a land that I know and love, filled with dark secrets and bright promises; it has not been my intention to imply that Brittany was, in the nineteenth century, any better or worse than any other place to live when one loved another woman.

What I have tried to do is envision the lives of several people who, each in her own way, lived out a destiny with authenticity, faithfulness, courage, and hope — the potential for which resides in all of us. I hope that, like me, it gives you dreams and visions, and courage to make them true.

New Haven
March, 1984

# Prologue 1897

# Mimi:

They came on a rainy morning in March. They came as men, with the anger of men; they came in self-righteousness and indignation. They came with their tools of terror: shovels and axes and sledgehammers and picks. And, among the crowd of people standing silently watching the destruction, not a single voice was raised in protest. Not even mine.

My fingernails had dug into the palms of my hands until they drew blood. How this could happen — how I could allow this thing to happen — was so incredible, it seemed to be a nightmare come true. The same feeling of fear and nausea and helplessness which tainted my worst dreams was suddenly, sickeningly real for me... especially the helplessness.

Philippa and Aurélie had been my people — in nearly every sense, my parents — and yet still I stood there, not defending them, not protesting, not praying, not even crying.

Marie was there. It was inevitable that she should be there, appropriate in a macabre, twisted sort of way. She was old now, nearly fifty years old; she had stopped caring, stopped loving, stopped feeling many years ago. In a place that accepts disappointment and disillusionment as an integral part of life, Marie had had more than her share of each; but is that an excuse for hatred? I found my own judgment too colored by emotion to be able to answer that — or even think about it.

I tried to picture her as she had been when Philippa and Aurélie knew her: young and healthy, in love, and happy — but it was too difficult for my imagination to evoke. Too many years and too much anger had misted over the image of the girl who had run laughing down to the sea to meet her young husband coming home.

Yet the friendship had been there. There were the meals they had all shared together, drinking wine and sitting up late over dirty dishes, talking and laughing. There were the moments of anxiety, when she had needed Aurélie and had leaned on her for support; there were the times of plenty, when she had knelt near Philippa in the village church and praised God for his bounty. She had lost her friends, just as she lost her husband; but the hatred had not come until later, when she felt that she had been betrayed. They had lied to her; and they had taken her daughter from her; and something in her refused to forgive, much less understand. Yet by that time there was only one person left to blame.

"Are you proud of them now?" Her voice was angry and bitter; and I could find no forgiveness for her, either. She had taken away more than a symbol, and she knew it. I turned and met her eyes.

"Yes," I said levelly. "As you would be, if you understood."

And then I ran away. Past the men with their awful noises, past the huddled group of women and children which silently parted for me to pass through, watching me with bright vicious eyes, past all of that, down — down to the sea, not to the wild forbidding cliffs where it had happened, but to the cove: the cove where they had first met. No one from the village ever went there; there, alone, could I find solace.

I felt safe in the cove, secure — I always had. I wanted so desperately to be able to cry, to scream at the heavens and the Deity who had fashioned them — why, oh God, why?

If I had been one of them, I could have done it. If I had been Philippa, I could have gone down to the village chapel and knelt among the flowers and the incense, and I could have prayed. If I had been Aurélie, I could have gone up to the clearing on the high cliffs, to the standing stones, and I could have wept. . . .

But I was neither Philippa nor Aurélie. I was only me, Mimi Aubray, their daughter, the outcast, the pariah — now, after today, the hunted and the hated. I had heard of people forced to leave their homes because of the fear and hatred of their neighbors, and now I could understand the feeling, red and hot and searing. I would be outcast because of Marie, and those who thought as she did — and because of all of us, Philippa and Aurélie, and myself.

The water was icy — it always was, until July or August. It was warm the day that Philippa and Aurélie met — late July, 1862. They had told me about it so often that the images came to my mind, crystal-clear, far more clear than they had been to the child who witnessed them. I was that child, too young to comprehend, too young to remember: I couldn't think of a time when Philippa was not there. It took that uncanny faculty of ours, that ability to become a part of each other's minds, for me to know what had happened that morning in the cove.

I closed my eyes and drew my cloak closer around me, the wool insulating me from the March chill. Aurélie would be the easiest, now — all that it required was some concentration. Aurélie, black hair shining in the sunlight as she brushed it out, tossing her head back, laughing... Aurélie, slipping away to her secret places, drinking from unknown streams of wisdom... Aurélie...

## *I* 1843-1858

# *Aurélie:*

*I* was born in November 1843 and christened Aurélie Madeleine Rousseau in the village church at Saint-Pol-des-Fougères. It was the same church in which my parents had been married; it was there, too, that my sister was married, that her baby was christened — and from which she was buried, when she was only twenty years old. The people of Brittany accept death as they do life: with a Mass and a bottle of Calvados and a shrug of the shoulders. Death is as inevitable as life — it is simply a matter of perspective.

I was happy when I was growing up. Saint Pol is a village like countless others scattered up and down the coast of Brittany, with its narrow cobbled streets and its old women dressed in black and its lilac trees which fill the air with their scent in the springtime. We always could tell when winter was finally over, when the lilacs appeared.

Saint Pol was Breton, too, in its ways: the fierce nationalism — not to France, but to Brittany — the dark superstitions, the strong mistrust of "foreigners" — anyone born outside our village, even if they came from only five kilometers away.

I was a resident of long standing, as had been my family. I knew by heart how many houses one passed on the way to school; I knew which streets were best for playing four-square; I knew that if one caught the baker's wife in good humor, one might obtain a croissant for nothing but a smile. I knew all of the people of the village and their ways; I knew their lives and habits, their fantasies and their sorrows. Just as they knew mine. . . to a point.

Fantasies were few in Saint-Pol-des-Fougères. The only thing in our lives, the focal point, the essence of our beings, required a strong hold on reality: it was the sea. The sea — source of life for all of us, of death for many of us. Most of the men were fishermen (the Leport family had a son in the Merchant Marine, but he was an exception); depending on the sea, with her moods and caprices, for their livelihood and that of their families. The sea gave and gave — and sometimes, to settle the score, she took.

It was a hard life for them; harder still for the women — women of steel, women of silence, who cooked and cleaned and spun. . . and waited.

Waiting. . . I grew up waiting. My father and my brothers were fishermen on Gerard Lehounnec's deep-sea trawler; they were away for days at a time. And Maman and my sister Chantale and I waited.

Always waiting, waiting and watching. . . walking the path up by the headland, worn by the footsteps of so many women, wives and widows of the sea. Scanning the horizon, imagining images of ships and husbands returning, with the gulls screaming death all about.

The waiting was the worst part of our lives; and it was what we did the most.

I remember the first time that I was aware of a boat not

coming back. Yann Bhelenc and his brothers were due back one evening when I was three or four years old; they never came. Lanterns, and cries in the night, with the thunder off in the distance and the rain pelting down.... I smelled fear that night, for the first time. After the shouting came the silence, and then the sounds of grief: the cries and the tears. Yann's new bride was nineteen when she put on the black widow's-weeds.

The sea gives and gives... but sometimes she has to take, as well. Still, it must have been hard for Sylvie Bhelenc to understand that, the night the sea took from her.

I went to school, to Mass on Sundays; I played with the other girls of the village — Marie, my best friend, and Yannick and Jeannine and Dominique — I didn't know then that I was different from them. I belonged there, one more little girl with black hair and dark eyes, playing four-square in the streets and reciting Lamartine at school and whispering scary stories to myself in the night. I was Aurélie Rousseau, no one special....

When I reached my teens, several things happened which changed my perspective on life more completely than I could ever have thought. First, I tasted the salt of my own grief when my father and brothers were claimed by the sea, in a storm which lasted for three full days. We were sure that they were gone, for wreckage washed up south of Saint Pol was identified as having come from their trawler. We were fortunate; there were women in Saint Pol who were never quite certain.

My mother was never the same after that, after Papa and the boys died. She had always been a little strange — silent, taciturn, not given to emotional outbursts; she never even wept at the memorial service for her husband and sons. She became stranger still: after that, the light which shone from her eyes was never totally sane.

We moved from our house in the village to one of the

deserted cottages up on the headland, where Maman would pace for hours, staring out at the ocean, mumbling words I couldn't understand. Down in Saint Pol there was talk — some said that she had gone mad, others claimed that she was a witch... it could have gotten dangerous, for such accusations are taken very seriously along the coast. But with time idle mouths found other things to gossip about. Jeannine Duroc eloped that spring with a foreigner, and my mother lost her gossip appeal after that.

I was glad to be up on the headland, away from the village; I could sit and watch the ocean, uninterrupted for hours at a time, and make up stories — I made believe that I was a beautiful princess imprisoned by a wicked king, and was waiting to be rescued. I never quite saw the prince who rescued me — perhaps I should have understood, then.

My sister Chantale did not go to live with us on the headland. By the time she was fifteen, everybody in the village knew that she would marry Christophe Aubray; she was barely sixteen when Papa and the boys were killed, and it seemed quite natural for Christophe to step in and fill the void that they had left in her life. It was not supposed to be done; but Chantale and Christophe were married three months after the wreckage of my father's boat was washed up on the Brittany coast.

I remember despising Chantale for what she was doing, leaving Maman and me alone, needing to be taken care of. I was fourteen, two years younger than she, blithely believing that I had the answers to everything. As, in a way, perhaps I did.

The wedding was quiet, and simple: our mourning dictated restraint. It was raining, so we couldn't dance in the streets as was the custom in our village, but the celebration went on nonetheless — champagne and confetti and laughter and music. Chantale's eyes were sparkling, she was as bright and bubbly as the champagne, and her gaiety was contagious. I found myself dancing and laughing — even dancing with Antoine Duroc, he of the enormous feet, who wanted to be courting me.

Maman and I walked home together from the wedding, silent, each of us preoccupied with her own thoughts. She finally broke the silence.

"Aurélie."

"Yes, Maman?"

"I will never see your wedding."

For a moment I said nothing. Perhaps she was depressed because of losing Chantale so soon after the others; perhaps she was merely making conversation — or, again, perhaps she did have some of the mysterious powers attributed to her. I didn't know.

We were climbing now, up the narrow path toward the cliffs. Below us the waves hissed and spluttered; the sea glowed as some phosphorescent brightness briefly illuminated its surface, then subsided into darkness. The wind had picked up again, tearing at our long skirts and our cloaks as it tore at the low scrub-like bushes bordering on the path, sending the clouds scuttling in front of the moon, moaning softly in a voice almost human in its intensity.

But it was not the wind which was making me shiver so suddenly, so uncontrollably.

"You will marry one from the north, a foreigner. I will be gone long before then, I will never see it with my eyes — but you understand, *ma mie*, that I do not require eyes to see these things. When the time is right, *ma petite*, you too may see things as I do. . . ." Her voice trailed away and she did not speak again that night.

As she spoke, her word had not been *étranger* — the masculine form of the word stranger, foreigner. Maman, with her eyes that saw past our realities, had said *étrangère:* the implication was there, already, for me to see — *étrangère*, a woman.

## II *1897*

# Mimi:

There was still mist over the sea. I sat on the cold sand, my arms clasped around my knees, tasting salt — salt of the sea, salt of my tears, they were all one.

How much time had elapsed — two seconds, two minutes, two hours? I had no idea. Aurélie had sometimes told me that time stands still when you leave your body, but I could never really tell. Just because you go back in time doesn't mean that the present doesn't go on without you, after all.

There were noises from up on the cliffs: sounds toppling down over the rocks, cascading down towards me, echoing eerily in the cove. I closed my eyes, as if by shutting off one of my senses I could will all the others to be still; closed my eyes against the fearful images those crashes evoked in my mind. The statue, the beautiful statue, in their hateful hands. . . .

I drew in a deep breath, telling my body to be still, not to be sick. My stomach settled slowly, and I finally opened my eyes. Mist, ocean, sand. . . nothing had changed.

It was a misty morning when Philippa had first come to the cove. I sometimes marvel at fate, at how much could be, and isn't, because it was not meant to be. If things were one way, they couldn't be another, and others would be otherwise. . . a step to the left or to the right, a moment too soon or a moment too late, a voice that speaks of death in the night. . . how many variables had to be present, had to be just so, for things to happen. And yet they *did* have to be just so, for the things *did* have to happen. I knew these things, for I was the granddaughter of a witch; but still I marvelled.

Philippa had come from the north, from Saint Malo. City of stone walls, of high ramparts, of dazzling ocean views. Philippa, the city lady — raised by nuns to be one of them, but with dreams that made her burst from her convent just as a captive bird flies from its confining cage.

A bird. . . yes, Philippa was like a bird, a beautiful bird with exotic plumage, pausing briefly in its flight to light in the cove, never dreaming that cove was to become its home.

Philippa was not one of us, she was a foreigner from the north; but for a reason I never understood, she alone had been accepted as one of us. Until today.

I closed my eyes again. Philippa had not been here to feel the heat of their hatred for her; and for that I was grateful. She never heard the voices raised against her. . . .

## III  1861-1868

# Philippa:

"*Agnus Dei, qui tollis peccata mundi, miserere nobis. Agnus Dei, qui tollis peccata mundi, miserere nobis. Agnus Dei, qui tollis peccata mundi, dona nobis pacem.*"

The voices rose with the incense, spiralling up towards the ceiling of the sanctuary, as if, through their sweetness and purity, they might transcend the stone and continue unrestrained to the heavens where they would surely find an Ear.

I wasn't singing. I knelt with the other girls in my class, the wool of my uniform skirt scratching my knees, feeling Régine Fariel squirming next to me. My eyes were on the flickering altar candles; I had always felt a strange attraction to fire. Fire and water, candles and the sea — these were the forces waging battle in my soul.

It was June, 1861, and I was sixteen years old. I was at morning Mass, as I had been every day since my memory began, since the night my mother died and I came to live at the convent. How many years ago had that been? Ten? Twelve? My memory had misted it over long ago, a time of grief and terror too horrible to remember.

The register in Sister Directress' office had my name on it, just as it had the names of all the other girls attending the convent school; and they were mostly similar.

"Philippa Genviève Chardonnais. Born October 19, 1845. Mother Frédérique-Aimée Ladoue Chardonnais, deceased. Father unknown."

Most of us were orphans — waifs of the world taken in by the nuns to be made into respectable bourgeois wives. Only a few had any relatives at all: Isabelle, my closest friend, had a grandmother; a few others had aunts, cousins, and so on. . . . It never particularly bothered me, having nobody of my own: the Sisters were mothers, aunts, cousins, grandmothers to us all. From the newest novice to the oldest stooped Mother, they knew us as we knew them; and we were a family.

I had never known any life but that of the convent. Masses, prayers, novenas, they were all a part of me. I prayed as I breathed, naturally and usually with little thought. Isabelle and I were known to be the renegades of the convent: we skipped classes, left prayers early, slid down banisters, stole the Sisters' habits off the clotheslines, rang bells at off hours, and were generally troublesome.

They put up with us, of course: we were family. But I knew, too, why convent floors always look so polished: I contributed a great deal to the cleanliness of the front hall as a result of my extracurricular activities.

Once a week I was sent with Sister Natalie to do errands in town. Sister fascinated me almost as much as did the city. She was a novice, and very young — twenty, I think. And beautiful. . . so beautiful. It was no wonder the nuns sent Sister Natalie to do the errands — shopkeepers would do anything for those eyes.

She was of the nobility, and say what one might about

class equality, that still made a difference. Especially to me: having lived all my life with those who are vowed to poverty, I longed for luxury. To think that Sister had given up so much — a title, a castle, rich young suitors, dances and parties and silk dresses — that, more than all the theology in the world, made me believe that there was indeed more to religious life than met the eye.

And Saint Malo! What a city! I loved it all: the narrow winding cobblestone streets, the ramparts by the sea, the houses jostling each other for space, the salty breeze which came in off the ocean. It was my home.

My father was English. That at least was known, that one piece of knowledge the only key my mother had whispered to the Sisters when she brought me to the convent, the only thing she would reveal of her past. She was found some days after, dead in a back street: I did not know for many years that she was found knifed to death. Apparently she did not deal with kind people, my mother; still, I forgave her, as Sister said I must, and said many prayers for the state of her soul.

I used to think about my father a good deal. He must have been a sailor — in a seafaring port such as Saint Malo it would stand to reason: a figure slipping off into the night without a word. And my love of the sea — it must have come from him, from one more at home on the rolling decks of a ship than in the staid streets of a city. He probably wasn't a bad sort, my father; perhaps he never even knew that I existed.

I thought and dreamed about seeing him one day. My own mother, the Mother Superior told me, was quite insistent that I be called Philippa — by no means a French or Breton name — and I would wonder, why that name? Was it because he was English? Was it a talisman, or perhaps a secret password she had arranged with my father: "You will know her, for she alone in Saint Malo is called Philippa"? I invented situations where he and I would meet; he was always kindly and gentle, and would take me to his ship and let me sail with him for

Liverpool or Southampton or London. . . . I studied the map of England with special interest, and I excelled in geography and English. Where did my roots lie? The North, Wales, Cornwall?

In the meantime, of course, I had to put up with the name Philippa.

I truly loved the sea. From the window of the study-hall in the convent — the highest window anywhere — one could see over the ramparts and glimpse the boats and the water. I could hear the merchants and the fishermen calling to one another, and it always thrilled me. I loved to read stories of pirates and sailors — and yet I loved learning, too.

So many contradictions. . . and, as the time for me to take my *baccalauréat* approached, my heart grew heavy with dread: I would have to do something.

I knew that once I obtained my *baccalauréat* two options would be open to me: I could either try to make my way in the world, as a governess or a seamstress or a lady's companion, and try to get married; or I could stay at the convent, take the veil, become a nun.

I didn't want to be a governess or a seamstress or a lady's companion — the only thing that I wanted to do was to go to sea, and my sex forbade that. I raged at the limitations placed upon me by my womanhood; I was angry and frustrated; but I couldn't change it. And the thought of marriage appalled me — giving up my will to that of some man? I should rather have been shot.

Still, the world was calling me. If it was God's will for me to become a Sister, then I would; but not until I had first tasted of His world.

I was given my diploma; I thanked Mother Superior and all of the Sisters; and I walked out of the convent into the sunlight.

It was springtime, and the air was hinting at warmth to come. People were out in the streets, all kinds of people, walking, laughing, enjoying their freedom. The pure joy and gaiety of it all was infectious, and I ended up smiling in return.

I found myself down on the docks. It was inevitable: the sea, irresistible as always, was calling me. I walked carefully lest I step on one of the many ropes coiled about, passing all the shops which cater to those who live on and by the water: ship chandlers, merchants of sails and rope, vendors of provisions. I walked, drinking it all in, watching and feeling and living. And, at length, I grew tired and simply sat on my suitcase, propped up against a wall in the sunlight, the drowsy warm sunlight, and the bustle and clatter of the docks faded slowly into the distance. . . .

I must have fallen asleep, leaning against the wall in the shadows, for when I awakened it was dark. Very dark. Frighteningly dark. The docks were suddenly dangerous, unfriendly, threatening. I got to my feet, picked up my suitcase, and strode away on legs that shook just a little.

From the shadows, shapeless voices accosted me: "Hey, honey, how much?" "Do you taste as good as you look?" "Come here so we can check the merchandise!" I know that my cheeks were flaming — not with embarrassment, but with anger — how *dare* they, I thought sullenly, how dare they make me go through all of this, because I wear a skirt? And still I walked on.

One of the voices had hands. They gripped me, suddenly and tightly, from behind. I screamed, dropping my suitcase, struggling for freedom. Behind me, the man only laughed. "So you like a little rough and tumble?" he grinned in my ear. I kicked him as hard as I could, then, and with a muffled moan of pain, he let me go. I didn't wait to see if he was all right; I ran.

There were more of them. I could hear their belches and their laughter, and then they were running after me, running faster than I could in my long skirts, their hands clutching at me from behind. I was pinioned again, this time against a wall, while one of them began to fumble with my cloak.

I screamed then, again and again, my voice echoing along the deserted expanses of wharf; I struggled until they cursed me. My cloak was thrown to the ground, and my shirt was ripped off, as well; someone was clumsily fingering my breasts. Oh God, oh God... my mind couldn't formulate a prayer, just the holy name, oh God.

He came from behind them, looming up suddenly in the darkness.

"Leave her alone!" It was a command, barked in a voice brooking no discussion. And, to my surprise, most of the men — there must have been five or six of them — immediately dropped back.

One still stood in front of me, attempting to raise my skirt. "It's Big Yves, Jacquot," one of the others hissed urgently at him, and he, too, immediately took hands off me.

"Go away. All of you. Away!" I faced my rescuer, my arms up, covering my bare chest as best I could, half fearful that he might have chased them away only in order to assail me himself.

I needn't have worried; he was not even looking at me. "Get your cloak on," he said, not unkindly, carefully averting his gaze from me. "We'd do better not to stay here now."

I stooped to gather up my fallen clothes and cover myself. My teeth were suddenly chattering.

"Monsieur, I— I wish to thank you," I finally stammered. "Were it not for you, I would surely—"

"Are you dressed, then?" It was no interruption; his mind was obviously elsewhere. "Then come along. We must not dally. Was that your case I spied, further on down?"

"Yes, monsieur. I dropped it when—"

"Yes, yes, of course," he interruped again. "I'll have it collected — if those ruffians haven't made off with everything of value in it. Was there much?" He looked straight at me then, a glint in his eyes. My rosary, I thought, a gift from Sister

Natalie. A picture painted at my first Communion. Things money couldn't replace; nothing of value.

"No, monsieur," I said meekly.

His mind was already elsewhere; he was watching the docks, and didn't look at me when next he spoke. "Best to be off, then, and soon." I stood still, and he swung around once more. "Come on, girl, don't stand there like you've lost you faculties. Come *on!*"

I went. Through narrow twisting alleyways, crossing over gutters where water dripped and rats scurried, up a frail wooden staircase into a room bright with firelight and cheery enough to make me smile. A woman was sitting beside the fire; she rose as we entered, her eyes glancing from the man to me.

"Yves?" she asked tentatively, and then waited.

The giant closed the door behind us and began pulling off his coat. "Found her down by the docks. Some of Pierre's boys found her first, though."

The woman's eyes went to my torn clothing, my disheveled hair; I could see them widen in understanding. "My poor child!" she exclaimed, putting her arm around my shoulder, pulling me closer to the fire. "What a time! What a nightmare! Thank God that Yves was there to help you — oh, dear Saint Mathilde, you've been hurt, child—"

I looked down at myself. "They are scratches, madame, nothing more. . . ."

"What nonsense, child. I'll put some ointment on them right away, it's the only thing to do — it will sting for a moment, my dear, but it will help, you'll see. Poor child. . . ." And she turned away to rummage in a cupboard in a far corner of the room.

Yves settled in front of the fire and began to remove his boots. "That Pierre," he commented to the room in general. "Something is going to have to be done. He'll be taking over the whole port in no time, you'll see."

The woman bustled back and began spreading some yellow sticky substance on my cuts; she was right — it hurt. "Well, dear," she said absently, "what do you propose to do?"

Yves shook his head. "Damned if I know, Mathilde."

"Yves! There is a young lady present! Really, my dear, men. . . . There. *C'est fini.*" She draped some soft woolen material around my shoulders, and replaced the ointment in the cupboard.

Yves, satisfied now that I was decently clothed, turned to me then. "Well, mademoiselle, perhaps now you will be so kind as to tell us who you are, and why you wander the docks at night like a—"

"Yves!" the woman cut in warningly.

". . . person who is lost," he finished smoothly, with a glance for his wife. "It's not healthy for a woman, as you have seen."

"Monsieur, I still have not thanked you properly for having come to me when you did. Truly, there are no words to express—"

He cut me off with a gesture. "It is nothing, mademoiselle. Once, I was unable to help one in time." Beside me, Mathilde made a sharp movement, but said nothing. "That one, mademoiselle, was our daughter. And she was killed. So perhaps I owed it to her, finding you tonight." He shrugged, and then looked at me directly. "Who are you, mademoiselle?"

I swallowed; I couldn't think why his questions made me nervous. "My name is Philippa Chardonnais, monsieur," I said meekly. "I'm from—"

"Chardonnais? That sounds familiar. Mathilde, where have I heard it before?"

His wife shrugged her shoulders. "I don't know, Yves. But the child is exhausted, she needs to sleep, leave your questions for the day, won't you? Now she will sleep!"

And I did, for eight beautiful luxurious hours.

Mathilde woke me in the morning, with freshly-baked crusty bread and hot steaming coffee. Yves was nowhere in sight.

"Eat, child," she urged me, sitting down by the fireplace — cold and empty now — and picking up some sewing.

I sat up with some difficulty, all of my muscles being sore, and attempted to do some justice to the breakfast. It wasn't difficult. As I did, Mathilde watched me anxiously.

"Have you anywhere to go now, child?" The question was abrupt, but not rude — she needed to know.

"No, madame."

"Oh! He was right, then. . . don't worry, we'll find someplace for you. Eat now."

And so I ate, thinking as I did that the timing was all wrong. Yves and Mathilde had needed a daughter, and I had longed for parents — but I was an adult now, too old to become the daughter they had lost.

It was then that I saw my suitcase by the door. "My case! You found it!"

"Of course, child. Pierre does not control the docks alone."

Yves came in an hour later, after I was washed and dressed properly again. He glanced at me, his eyes widening in surprise; I wondered how I had looked the night before, to cause such an expression now. But he merely said, "So, Mademoiselle Chardonnais, now we will take a walk."

I glanced at Mathilde, who nodded, and I followed him into the sunlight of the street.

"Impossible to talk around that woman," Yves announced, setting off at a strong pace. I followed as best I could. "Married her once, I'd marry her again, but impossible to talk around her." I couldn't think of an answer for that, so I remained silent.

"Chardonnais." His voice was abrupt. "Are you related to Aimée Chardonnais, then?"

I stopped and stared at him. "My mother? You knew my mother?"

He sighed, taking my arm and steering me around a vege-
table cart in the street. "Yes, you would be. You've that look of
her about you — except for your eyes. Honest eyes, you've got.
Aimée didn't. She—" He broke off and looked away. From
what I remembered, from what nuns had told me, I thought I
understood.

"My mother was a prostitute, monsieur, wasn't she?"

He looked startled at my frankness. "Your mother, mademoiselle, had a very hard life. She survived longer than many
others did." His tone changed abruptly. "Was that why you
were at the docks last night, trying to find your mother?"

"No, monsieur. I know that my mother is dead." We had
entered the park now, the one Sister Natalie and I used to walk
through on the way to market. We sat together on a bench. He
was still watching me. "I myself was raised by the Sisters at
the Visitation Convent on the rue des Arènes. I went
because—" I hesitated, but he merely waited, so I went on, "I
don't expect that you will understand, monsieur, but I will try
to explain. All of my life I have loved the sea, longed for it —
they say that my father might have been a sailor. I — many
times I have wished to be a man, to be accepted on a ship, to
go to sea, to be part of that life: it's what I want. I— I only left
the convent yesterday, monsieur, and I needed to be close to
the sea, and I fell asleep. . . ." For the first time I dared to look
at him. "Is that a terrible thing, monsieur?"

He did not answer, but we began walking again, back
through the twisting streets with their tantalizing glimpses of
the ocean, sparkling blue in the sunshine. Yves was deep in
thought, and I walked silently beside him, trying vainly to
divine his thoughts. At length we arrived at the docks, bustling and busy in the morning light. I suppressed a shiver; but
it was not the same place it had been in the night.

"Tell me, mademoiselle, how strong are you?" Yves' voice
cut into my thoughts. I blinked.

"Strong, monsieur? I do not understand—"

He gestured impatiently. "Were it not for your sex, you could work on a ship?"

"Oh, yes, monsieur, I could. I know I could. But—"

He was already walking away. I ran to join him.

"Look down there at that boy — the one fixing a rope, can you see him?"

"The one in the striped shirt, monsieur?"

"Yes, that one. He's been on board the *Juste à Temps* for nearly a year now — galley-boy, you understand, nothing too important, but he's on a ship."

I waited politely. I had no idea what he was driving at.

"That boy, mademoiselle, is as much a man as you are."

I gaped at him. "Monsieur—"

He smiled. "And you thought that you were the only one to catch this fever, mademoiselle. A strong back and a steady stomach is all that is asked. Papers are easily forgotten when there is work to be done, and she—" he nodded towards the slim figure on the pier, "is one of the hardest working of them all."

There was a moment of silence. He looked away. "If you wish to do this thing, mademoiselle, I will help you. Last night it was for my daughter, and that is settled. I still owe one for your mother."

"But you said—"

"What? What did I say? She had no choices, mademoiselle, your mother. No choices — about her life, about you, about even her death perhaps." He cleared his throat. "Long ago, mademoiselle, when I was a young man, before I met Mathilde who I married, I knew your mother. I loved her, mademoiselle. I wanted to marry her. She laughed at me, told me to pay. . . . That is over, I could never help Aimée. Perhaps I can help her daughter instead."

There was a film over my eyes. "Monsieur—"

"That is all. We have much to do."

# _Mimi:_

_I_ rose then, carefully brushing the sand from my skirt. Aurélie, Philippa, their names mingled in my mind, as did their faces, young and beautiful and laughing. Always laughing. There is good to be found in life, Philippa always told me, you have only to look a little, and laugh.

I remember when she first told me about the terrible night on the docks, right after she left the convent, of her concern that I understand that there is evil and violence in the world as well as goodness and bravery. She spoke so much of Big Yves who had rescued her that night, of his warmth and love and kindness. What was his last name? I don't think that she ever knew. But she prayed for him, and for his wife Mathilde, every day of her life, kneeling in the village chapel which always smelled of incense and lilies.

The wind was really chilly now, and I pulled my cape

more tightly around me. Above, the clifftops were silent; it was over. People may come to watch such a thing, feeling a thrill at the sensational and the unexpected, but they also have their lives to get on with: bread to be baked, fish to be caught — no matter how heart-wrenching something is, life does flow placidly on.

For me, too. I felt suddenly, absurdly, small and alone there on the beach. All of my people were gone: Aurélie and Philippa, who were my parents, and Adèle, who had been my love... and I alone was left to live on the headland in the house which had seen so much life, and now stood empty and haunted by the images of its past.

The path to the headland was steeper than usual... could I be getting old, then? Only thirty-eight; hardly ancient. Thirty-eight years ago I was born in this village, to a woman who I never knew. I lived in the house on the headland with two women who loved me and cared for me and died without saying good-bye to me; and I loved a woman who shared her life and vibrancy and delight in the world with me until last year when she, too, died without saying good-bye.

Why should that have bothered me so? That is how life is: filled with the unexpected, so that we never know when to say hello or good-bye, much less who to say it to. My mother scarcely had time to say hello to me, and never thought to say good-bye; and I can hardly hold it against her.

It was a miracle, they all said, that I did not take my mother's life when I was born. Everyone but Aurélie knew that her sister was dying, and that childbirth might well be the final effort of her life. And Aurélie — one couldn't blame her, really, for not knowing that my mother was dying.

She had concerns enough, just then, with her own mother.

## V 1858

# Aurélie:

*J* discovered the menhirs the same day I learned that Chantale was to have a baby.

There are parts of the cliff which children never explore: not because of any danger — that would never have stopped anybody — but because there is some mysterious unspoken taboo concerning them.

Like all of the village children, I had respected these taboos, afraid of the vague veiled threats which were the consequence of disobedience. Even when I was very small, long before Papa and the boys died, I heard stories of sea serpents living in the caves below the cliffs; I listened in awe to the stories of the little boy who one day wandered up past the headland at the full moon and was never heard from again.

Since I had come to live on the headland, though, social pressures had lessened, and I was free to explore wherever I wished without people talking about it. I was the daughter of Iseut *la folle*, after all, and a witch's child must be immune to the spirit world.

I started taking long walks — originally, because I couldn't stand staying in the house with my mother. She seemed to grow stranger daily. She had taken to sitting for hours on end staring into space, rousing herself from time to time to speak enigmatic words. I didn't understand, and so I fled.

Later, though, my walks seemed to satisfy some deep need inside of me — one I had never known existed — and I found myself drawn away from the house every time my chores permitted. It was as though there was something out there, calling me, daring me to come further.

So I walked, listening to the screams of the gulls as they wheeled and careened about the clifftops, their raucous cries piercing the wind. And I listened, too, for the voice within me, which was telling me which way to go.

That day I had gone up past the headland, where the ground dipped down and low scrub bushes — which alone could survive on the clifftops — were gradually replaced by slight trees and then by a thicket. Here was the boundary, past which it was forbidden to go. I went.

The thorns caught and tugged at my skirt; they scratched my hands and cheeks — yet I went on. Beyond the thicket were more trees: strange trees, with grotesque, stunted trunks twisting this way and that, as if even the trees themselves in this place were cursed. I felt some misgivings, then; but the voice was still there, whispering in my mind, and I went on. Beyond the trees, there was nothing: just the gently sloping grass.

It was then that I saw the menhirs.

I knew what they were, of course: standing stones, megaliths, left behind by some forgotten people or god; the coast of Brittany was dotted with them. Yet, standing alone as I was in the fading twilight (why had I chosen to come so late in the day?), with the mist beginning to come in off the sea, I saw only massive grey giants, grouped together as if for some secret rite or sacrifice.

Sacrifice was probably closer. Among the stones was a dolmen, a slab of rock laid horizontally across four low-standing stones: almost certainly an altar. I stood shivering, looking at the stones in the grey light, feeling the stillness, the absolute silence, nothing moving or breathing, not a whisper of wind — I suppose that the trees cut it off — as if everything which had ever lived in that place was now dead.

Behind me, suddenly, came a scream. I gasped and whirled around, losing my footing as I did, stumbling and sliding down the slight incline, stopping my tumble beside one of the great stones. From the trees, now, came nothing but silence; it had merely been the cry of a gull. As if to confirm this thought, another cry — this time further off — answered the first one and was in its turn answered by others.

I took a deep breath, the first in minutes, then drew back again as I realized where my panic-stricken fall had taken me. For better or for worse, I was there.

I sat like that for a moment, matching the stillness of the place, breathing the air as might an animal, questing it for danger, seeking information. Common sense told me to leave: darkness was not far away — it was already more murky than it had been when I had first come, and the mist had penetrated the trees and was now weaving in and out of the tall unmoving figures.

Or were they unmoving? I watched one closely, every nerve on edge, and it seemed to be almost alive. . . . No, Aurélie, I said fiercely to myself, that is nothing, a trick of the light, stone cannot more. Leave, leave now, before your nervousness turns to terror.

And yet still I sat there, knowing that this was the place to which I had been drawn all along; knowing, too, that if I left now I should never come back.

Suddenly the place was alive. There were whispers all around me, whispers carried on the mist, whispers from the stones, from the grass on which I sat. Whispers of those who stood watch... and I knew, somehow, that I was safe, that the whispers were meant for me, that nothing here would hurt me. I don't know how I knew this; I don't even know if, had they been there, anyone else could have heard the murmurs: perhaps they had been inside me all along. That really does not matter, of course: it is all the same.

With darkness falling, I rose, clutching the stone for support — it was no longer frightening to touch. Something was still drawing me, urging me to stay, not to go... but I had left my mother alone. Resolutely, I turned and walked back toward the stunted trees: it was time to go.

For some reason which I didn't understand, I turned before I left, and said, quite clearly: "I'll be back. You know that I will."

Whatever god dwelled in the place must have been satisfied with that small offering, for I was able to go without fear at my back.

There were lights on at the house in the headland when I got back. My shawl was drenched with the mist and the sea spray, and I pulled it from my shoulders as soon as I entered. Chantale and Christophe were there.

"Where have you been? It's well past nightfall." That was Chantale, sounding curiously maternal. "Out walking," I said briefly and went to kiss my mother. Her eyes were wide, the pupils dilated; but she smiled and returned my kiss nonetheless — and when Chantale began to say something else to me, Maman raised her head and said, "Enough. Leave the child alone," and Chantale, surprised, did so.

I sat down by the fire and pulled out my sewing — the skirt I had ripped on a gorse bush the week before. Christophe was smoking a pipe, which smelled terrible; he seemed uncomfortable, getting up every few minutes, walking restlessly to the window or the fireplace.

"What brings you here at night?" I asked at length, more to break the silence than out of real interest. "I'm told it's thought to be bad luck."

Christophe took up the conversational offering, such as it was. "That's nonsense," he said gruffly. "There's no such thing as bad luck — not about a house. The path is dangerous in the dark, that's all."

I smiled. "So the path is dangerous. Maman and I manage it, but I suppose that we're surer on our feet than most."

"Aurélie!" That was Chantale, always the mediator, anxious to preserve peace. "He meant nothing ill by it."

"Perhaps not." I shrugged my shoulders — my brother-in-law's opinion mattered little to me. "Does everyone in the village find the path so dangerous, then, that they cannot come?"

Christophe glowered at me. "I know nothing of what the village thinks. Nor do I care."

Chantale said, "I'm pregnant."

For pure shock value, the effect was complete. I looked at her curiously. She certainly didn't look pregnant, but perhaps that wasn't necessary. I decided not to ask her how she knew; and looked instead at my mother for her reaction. Her eyes were unfocused and she was clearly not in the room with us.

"Are you glad?"

It was Christophe who answered. "Of course we're glad," he snapped. "What else?" He turned to his wife, hand outstretched: "Come, Chantale. It's time we left."

Chantale flung me a wan smile, then cast a doubtful look towards my mother.

"Is she all right, Aurélie?"

"Of course. She's happier when she leaves, I think, than when she's conscious."

Chantale frowned. "Does she—" but Christophe took her arm then, and she gave up. "Good-bye, Aurélie. Come down soon to see me, won't you?"

"When I can, Chantale. Good-bye."

The door slammed behind them, and they were away, down that dangerous path to the village. I sat there for some time in silence, my needle flashing regularly in the firelight, feeling the warmth and peace and goodness of home. Not understanding, never understanding, why my sister had chosen Christophe over this....

The minutes ticked away softly from the clock on the mantelpiece. It was the one thing of value that we possessed, that clock: it came from my grandfather, who had purchased it in Paris. The hands were of chased gold, and there was blue enamel outlining the characters. All the time I knew belonged to that clock: good, peaceful minutes....

"You were up at the menhirs." My mother's voice broke through my thoughts and I straightened with a start.

"I'm sorry, Maman. What did you say?"

"You were up by the menhirs this evening."

"Yes, Maman, I was. How did you know?"

She dismissed the question with a perfunctory wave of her hand. "I saw you."

"Were you up there, too? I never saw—"

"You will understand some day that there are many different ways of seeing," she interrupted. "Eyes..." her voice trailed off, and I thought for a time that she had lapsed back into her trance; but then she started speaking again.

"You will go again, to the place of the stones. Listen to what they will say to you — they have so much to tell you, *ma petite*, so much to teach. And you will need all that they can give you."

"Maman — did you ever go, you, to the menhirs?"

Her eyes focused on me for a brief moment. "Naturally. They are of the earth — earth and fire, air and water, those are the only true sources of knowledge...." She straightened, then, in her chair; and when she spoke again her voice had lost its dreamlike quality. "You must understand, Aurélie, that if you keep going there people will talk about you. They will not understand."

"Who will know, Maman?"

She smiled. "There are no secrets here, child. The wind will carry your name... oh, it will be known, you will see. People say that I am strange, Aurélie. Perhaps they will think the same of you, in time."

I stared at her. Maman, sweetly oblivious Maman, conscious of the village gossip? I swallowed and said quickly, "It does not matter to me, Maman. I need to go up to the stones. I don't quite know why."

"There is no need for you to explain. I understand. And you will learn, child, far more than they ever taught you in that silly school down in the village."

She was silent, then, and I picked up my sewing again. Later, as I was moving about, tending the fire, preparing for bed, she suddenly called my name.

"Yes, Maman?"

"Chantale's child will be a girl. She—" She seemed to be searching for words for a moment, and I waited, but she shook her head in frustration. I knew what she felt: sometimes mere words are insufficient to tell somebody else all the images which go through one's mind.

"Come to bed, Maman."

She let me put her to bed, like a small child herself, muttering something about visions and Chantale having no use for them. "Perhaps her child. . . ."

"Hush, Maman."

She fell asleep almost at once. But I was awake for hours, listening to the wind howl outside the door. The pounding of the latch matched exactly that of my heart.

## VI *1861*

# *Philippa:*

"*Philippe!* Hey! Grab this rope, boy!"

The voice came from above me, out of the darkness: I recognized it as that of Lucien, the second-in-command of the *Sea-Star*. He rarely spoke to me at all, so I scrambled to do his bidding.

"Tie it up well down there!" His footsteps were gone, and once again all that I could hear was the sound of the waves and the wind. I made an expert knot — oh, how many blisters had it taken me to learn those knots! — and left it.

The *Sea-Star* was my home now, the only home I had had for the past four months; and by now I had had time to settle down into the role which Big Yves had given me that brisk morning in Saint Malo. I was Philippe Chardonnais, deckhand, sixteen years old, and an eager and able worker. To all intents and purposes, Philippa Chardonnais, student at the Convent of the Visitation, was no more.

Mathilde hadn't liked it, not one bit. "Why you're doing this, child," she spluttered, "I'll never know. Why, with your looks, you could marry well—"

"I don't want to marry, madame," I replied. "I want to go to sea."

"Nonsense, this idea of yours. And you, Yves, carrying on as if it were the most normal thing in the world for her to do, I don't understand—"

"You don't have to," he said calmly. "And it is."

"Oh, stubborn, the two of you. And now I've got to cut off all of your beautiful hair, you say, and what a waste that is. Nearly down to your skirt, child, aren't you going to miss it, even?"

"Not if it's what is holding me back."

"Holding you back! Holding her back, dear Saint Mathilde! What an idea! What nonsense!"

"Cut her hair, Mathilde," Yves said, "or I shall have to do it myself."

Once again I found myself standing in the brilliant sunshine on the docks of Saint Malo, waiting while Yves talked with some formidable figure in a dark blue jacket.

"... the boy has never worked before, not on a ship, but my sister-in-law, his mother — may God rest her soul — told me that he's a fine, able lad, and keen to work."

The other looked at me as if judging a piece of meat. I tried to appear as nonchalant as possible, while inside me my heart hammered like a captive bird trying to escape.

"How old are you, boy?" The captain was speaking to me.

"Sixteen, monsieur," I managed to croak.

"Hmm. All right, then, but it's a favor to you, Yves. The moment he's not quick enough—"

"He'll be quick." Yves was looking directly at me as he spoke. "You'll not be sorry."

I drew myself up under his gaze. "No, sir," I said softly, "you won't."

And so began my life on the *Sea-Star*, barely a fortnight after I left the Convent of the Visitation. I was quick, as Yves had said that I would be: I didn't let him down. Gradually the gruffness of Captain Lemieux was replaced by grudging acceptance — if a captain can be said to entertain any thoughts at all about a mere deckhand — and I was well-liked among the crew. The older men, delighted at what they perceived as my innocence, regaled me with bawdy stories of women ("You'll see, boy, when you are older....") at which I forced myself to laugh.

Best of all, no one knew about me.

We were making the Channel run frequently then, transporting cargo and the occasional passenger from Le Havre and Brest and Saint Malo — but especially from Le Havre — over to Southampton. I grew to love Le Havre, as I had once loved Saint Malo, though for different reasons. Le Havre, where it was always raining, was a real working seaport. And the excitement of being part of that never really left me.

It was Southampton that intrigued me the most. And, paradoxically, it was there that I almost gave myself away. We would be in port for two or three days between runs, especially if bad weather threatened, and the first time it happened I set off on my own to explore the city. I hadn't gone far, though, when an English sailor, carrying a heavy keg on his shoulder, jostled me. "Sorry, lad," he called over his shoulder and, without thinking, I automatically responded, "Not at all."

Beside me, someone made a sharp movement, and I looked up to see François Leclerc, bosun's mate on the *Sea-Star*. He was staring at me in the most disquieting manner.

"Well, Chardonnais," he said slowly, "I didn't know that you spoke English. Where did you learn that?"

I gaped at him. I had spoken English to the sailor — in a

moment I was transported back to Sister Marie des Anges's English class, sitting beside the open window with the sun streaming in. "Mademoiselle Chardonnais, please conjugate the verb 'to trace,' in English, for your classmates." I had devoured English as no other subject, thinking that I was after all half English, that I should know my father's language.

And now — Philippe Chardonnais, the cousin from the farm that Yves had invented, who had had no formal schooling, was suddenly speaking English.

"I learned it, monsieur, from the priest in our village. He said I had an — an aptitude for languages, monsieur."

Leclerc believed me, and told the captain, who was pleased. "Useful, that, Chardonnais," he said, "we'll bear it in mind." I resolved then to be more careful.

And so my life settled into a pattern: so many days at sea, so many days in port. It was a wonderful life, and as I stood alone at the stern of the ship, watching the wake and the gulls wheeling above it, I felt peace: I'd not have exchanged that life for any other.

All was well for Philippe Chardonnais, deckhand on the *Sea-Star*. Until winter. Until the winter came, and I caught that terrible, racking cough. . . .

# VII 1897

# *Mimi:*

*I* was coughing slightly as I opened the door to the house. It was nothing — just particles of dust in the wind which had caught in my throat. I closed the door hurriedly behind me and turned in relief, crossing the room to stir up the fire which had faded in my absence to glowing embers.

It was then that I saw the portrait.

It was a portrait of Adèle, hanging over the fireplace as it had for the past ten years. It had been painted in Saint Malo — we had gone up there to spend the day, a sort of holiday for the two of us, far from the curious eyes of the village. We had eaten lunch together, sitting in the sunshine on one of the high rampart walls, tossing the apple cores to the birds — there were seagulls whirling and screaming all around us. Mostly I remember the laughter that we shared that day. . . and the old man who had offered to paint Adèle's portrait for her. She was so embarrassed: people always responded that way to her, to her prettiness. I sat on the wall, warmed from the sun, and watched him draw her face on the canvas; and we giggled and chattered all the while. And then we brought the portrait home with us, up to the headland, and nailed it up over the fireplace, behind Aurélie's little clock with the chased gold hands. Somehow, I knew that Philippa and Aurélie would have liked the addition to their house.

I straightened up, slowly, from the fireplace, staring in horror at the portrait. Adèle's laughter had been silenced: for the picture was ripped, slashed across her face, with cruel jagged edges. It was so real, so terrifyingly real, that for a moment I almost expected the blood to pour out of the canvas onto my hands, drip onto the floor. . . dear God, what more could they do? Hurt upon hurt upon hurt, and no time for healing. Adèle had died, and now, just as the likeness of Philippa and Aurélie had crashed into oblivion, so too had this image of the woman I had loved been wrenched from me. Adèle. . . I reached out a hand, tentatively, to touch the ripped canvas, but pulled it away again as if it had been burned. There are some things that a person cannot do.

I had sat quietly on the sand, seeking solace in my visions, healing myself the only way that I knew how; and they had come here then, to hurt me more, to kill the last part of me that still struggled for life.

Marie — it had to be Marie. But could she? I was sure that Marie would do whatever she could to hurt me; that was given. But destroy this likeness of her daughter — could she really go that far? To take a knife and plunge it into the eyes which matched her own, into the smile that she, too, had loved?

Of course she had. Marie was the only person in the village who would have dared to set foot in this house; everyone else believed it to be cursed, to bring bad luck — the villagers all made the sign against the evil eye every time they even had to go near it. Only Marie, Marie with her blind rage, would not hesitate to come through that door. To hurt me, the way that she would have turned on Adèle if she had known when Adèle was still alive.

I was almost glad that Adèle had died. She had loved Marie with all of her heart: she would have grieved to see such a terrible change come over her mother. She had not told Marie the entire truth, of course, about why she had come to live with me; but nor had she lied when she said that we were close friends and that she simply did not choose to marry. Marie, in turn, adored Adèle and never questioned her decision. . . until after Adèle died and she learned that we shared more than friendship. And Marie became a woman filled with hatred and violence.

Yet I knew what they said in the village, how they commiserated with her, sympathized: poor woman, it's no wonder, the terrible burden that she bears, the pressures that she is under. . . .

I turned, abruptly, from the fireplace and bolted for the door. Suddenly, I needed to be sick.

## VIII 1859

# Aurelie:

It happened on a Friday, so perhaps there is something, after all, in that Catholic mythology, linking death with that day of the week. I didn't know.

All I knew was that I had been up with the menhirs, as I was frequently, thinking and listening. And when the voice inside me said, "Go home — now," I unquestioningly obeyed. The voices were always right.

As I picked my way through the gorse bushes, I suddenly had a vision of my mother, lying alone on her bed, grasping her chest with one of her thin, chalky hands. I began to run.

By the time I reached the house, she was dead.

I sat with her for a long time, wishing with all my strength that she would communicate something to me, I didn't know what, something, anything, tell me why she left so suddenly, tell me what I should do. But she was silent, and the voices inside my head were silent, too, so I pulled the cover up over her head because I had read in books that that was what one was supposed to do, and I pulled my cloak off the peg by the door, and picked my way down the path to the village.

Marie's house was the first one that I came to, lying as it did on the outskirts of Saint Pol. Marie had always been my very best friend while I lived in the village; our lives were different now, for she was married (her baby Jean-Luc was born just four months after her wedding; that was why she married so very young), but we were still close, and if I had to tell this to anyone, it might as well be Marie.

She had been cooking, and her face was flushed as she came out of the kitchen in answer to my knock. "Aurélie!" Her voice was delighted. "I'm so glad you came! Come in, don't just stand there, like a visitor! I'll get some cider... there. Now sit down — oh, just a moment, now, I'll get the baby, he's due to be up at any moment now, and that way we won't be interrupted...."

Her voice trailed off as she disappeared into another room, and a moment later she returned with Jean-Luc balanced on her hip. I looked at him curiously: some detached part of my mind noted that I had never seen an uglier baby. Perhaps babies were supposed to look like that.

"I've seen quite a bit of Chantale — she's due to have her baby quite soon, isn't she, poor soul...."

"Poor soul?" I couldn't help but ask the question, although back in the darkness of my brain someone kept screaming: Maman is dead! Maman is dead! I didn't know who was shouting like that, but I wished that they'd be quiet: it was giving me a headache.

"Didn't you know?" Marie looked surprised. "Well, I suppose that you wouldn't, isolated like that up on the headland. She hasn't been well, you know, and the doctor's concerned about her having a baby on top of being so sick already. Doesn't your mother know?"

"My mother is dead." There, I had finally said it, in a voice that even to my own ears was curiously flat and muffled. Maybe it just sounded that way inside my head. I looked at Marie to see what she'd say.

"Your — oh, Mother of God, here I am rattling on. Aurélie, oh, I'm so sorry. . . ." She put the baby down on the floor and knelt beside my chair and put her arms around me. "Aurélie, oh, I don't know what to say." I sat very still, letting her words wash around me, a river of chatter flowing around me, curiously soothing. . . .

She had asked a question. "What did you say?"

"When did it happen?"

"Today. I don't know what time."

"Have you told anybody else yet?" I shook my head, and she became brisk, in control of the situation. "Well, we must get Dr. Lehecneau, right away, and I suppose Monsieur Benoit, as well. You stay here, Aurélie, drink some cider, I'll see to it."

I thought that she was going to leave Jean-Luc there, on the floor, but she cast a doubtful look in my direction and picked him up before going out the door. I started to laugh. What did she think I was going to do, smash a baby against the wall in a fit of grief?

I sat very still, until the shadows began to lengthen in the room. The men would be coming home soon, except for those doing night-fishing.

There was a step in the doorway, then, and Chantale came in. She was very big with her pregnancy now, and had to hold on to the doorframe for support.

"Aurélie!"

I stood up at last, turning to face my sister. I drew in a deep breath; truly she did look ill. "Chantale—"

And then she was suddenly in my arms, and we were holding each other, and she was sobbing, the tears trickling down her face and onto my neck, cold and wet. I held her and let her cry, and patted her back occasionally, and then the sobs grew more and more muffled, and at length she drew slightly away from me and began hunting for her handkerchief.

"Here." I handed her mine, and she managed a smile, brave through the tears. "Thanks, Aurélie."

She sat down, heavily and with difficulty, and began to talk. "The doctor was just up there. He said that she had a heart attack."

"I know. I saw it."

Her eyes widened. "You mean that you were there?"

"No. I was up on the headland, further off. That's why I went home: I saw her having the attack." She looked at me blankly, and I began to wish that I hadn't opened up this particular part of myself to my sister. "In my mind, I saw it, Chantale. I see things, sometimes, just the way that Maman does — that Maman used to."

That started her crying again, the mention of Maman in the past tense, and I waited, but suddenly she wasn't crying at all, she was screaming and clutching at her stomach and falling to the floor.

I don't remember what I did. I must have done all the correct things, summoned the doctor, because he was there, and so was Christophe, and Marie was back, and Chantale was having her baby there in the middle of Marie's kitchen floor.

I stood outside the door, breathing the night air, praying to whatever god would listen that she might be all right — perhaps even praying to Maman, I don't know. Why not? People pray to saints, after all, and saints are dead people. Besides, Maman would certainly care more about Chantale than would any other dead person who ever knew her. . . .

It seemed years before Marie came out of the house and put her arm around my shoulders. "It's all right, Aurélie. She had the baby, it's a girl, and they're both all right."

She was christened in the village church a week later. Madeleine Iseut Aubray was the name that they gave her, and it was oddly satisfying to me to know that the names were from our family — Madeleine from me, Iseut from my mother — and not from Christophe's.

I don't think that Christophe cared: he was too worried about Chantale. It was a good thing that I, as godmother, was holding the baby during the christening, for in the middle of it Chantale fell silently to the floor in a faint, and after that day she was in bed a great deal of the time.

I stayed mostly to myself after that — it seemed that the things which were happening inside my head were more interesting than the trivial affairs of Saint Pol. Once, sitting with my back leaning against one of the standing stones, I actually felt myself being a part of Maman — only during a different time, when she was alive, of course. I saw the house we lived in down in the village, and Papa and the boys coming in late for supper, and a little girl in the corner alone who I recognized to be myself. The experience frightened me, but I tried it again and again — all that I had to do, really, was concentrate — and learned all sorts of things that I had never dreamed of.

Once, too, I saw something which I didn't understand, and which frightened me out of proportion. There was a cliff, and some sort of monument on it, except that suddenly the monument was falling over the side of the cliff. I saw it fall slowly, in slow motion as it were, and then I saw all the people standing behind it, and felt — how strange! — such hatred from those people that I was really disturbed.

I still went down to Saint Pol for Mass and shopping, and to see Chantale and my friend Marie. The baby was pretty, and I sometimes played with her when my sister wasn't feeling well. Christophe invited me to move into their house with them in order to care for Chantale and Madeleine — or Mimi as we all began to call her — but I couldn't leave the headland, not even for them.

Marie was pregnant again; so many of my friends were at

that time, as if getting married and making babies was all that existed for them. Antoine Duroc was still very interested in me, and the village priest encouraged me to marry him; but still I waited. I was only sixteen, there was time.

And so the months passed. There were good times, times of plenty; then the gales of autumn brought scarcity and fishing boats that did not return. Marie's brother Philippe was one who didn't; and there were others, too — it was a hard winter.

I went down to the village more and more frequently then, sometimes bringing Mimi back to the cliffs to stay with me for some days, as Chantale was weaker and weaker. There was fear in my heart now, and I didn't go to the standing stones: I was too afraid of my visions, afraid that I would see another one of my family die.

I needn't have worried: she died quietly in her sleep in 1861. Her daughter Mimi was two years old; Chantale was only twenty.

Mimi came to live with me after that. I was eighteen, a strong grown woman, able to care for myself and for the child. We buried Chantale beside Maman in the churchyard, and Christophe left the next day: we never saw him again.

Marie's child was a girl, named Adèle; sometimes I took Mimi to the village to play with Jean-Luc and Adèle, and on occasion Marie would venture up to the headland. Not often; but she was the only one who came. My mother's shadow lay heavy on the house.

I took Mimi on long walks with me, becoming a parent for the first time, trying out the limits of our relationship. I didn't take her up to the standing stones, though: if that was meant to be, it was for later.

One day we walked down to the cove — it was an easy path, so we went there often — and we sat on the sand in the fresh springtime sun, and made sand castles and giggled at each other and I sangs songs to her.

Mimi had climbed up into my lap, playing with my face

and hair, and I happened to glance over her head to the ocean. It was impossible, but there was a storm out there: the waves were high and I could vaguely discern the shape of a ship lying a little off the coast, a vague form perceived through the mist and driving rain. A figure was standing on the deck, and, as I watched, it dove off into the sea.

I blinked my eyes, and the sea once more became calm, the sun shining benevolently on it, and I realized that it had been another vision, even if I wasn't by the standing stones.

I shivered in the warm sun and, despite Mimi's loud protests, went back home. I was too afraid of seeing more.

# _Mimi:_

_I_ had taken the picture down, and set it behind my bed: Adèle's face ripped and disfigured and crying out with the injustice of it all.

I took out my writing, and settled down with the paper on the kitchen table to work: but it stayed blank while the words whirled round and round in my head. It was no good: the thoughts were too wild and violent to allow themselves to be confined to mere words and phrases and sentences; and I gave it up.

The present was unbearable: only in the past could I find any peace.

It was easy, standing there at the window, looking out over the headland to the line where the ocean met the horizon, to feel the past overcoming me. This was the house where I had lived as a child, when the foreigner came into our lives, when Adèle and I had played and run screaming over the hills, when Aurélie had dreamed her dreams and Philippa had refused to accept limitations.

There were the dark times, of course. It's so easy to see the days of the past as sunlit and pure: a time of innocence where every task was clear and every decision easy. There is no time more difficult to live in than the present; our damnation is that it is the only time we can ever possess.

But the past, too, was difficult. I might not have understood, then, just how difficult it was for Aurélie and Philippa — but I understood it the night that I came home to a house filled with people and none of them my parents: I understood the depth of a pain that can formulate no words or grief, accept no words of comfort. Only Adèle could speak to me that night. . . .

The night that Philippa didn't come back. That horrible night when rain lashed the house and Aurélie ran out into it, pacing the headland in the wind and the rain, crying for the visions that never came. And deciding, deciding in the darkness and cold that life for her couldn't go on without Philippa. . . . And she never told me good-bye.

I shook myself and turned away from the window, from the images of death. The torn jagged edges of Adèle's portrait had been too evocative: the thought of Aurélie, lying broken on the sharp piercing rocks, as they had found her the next day, and me with them, surfaced far too easily and readily. The sound of my screaming had echoed off the cliffs and out over the sea: and I could still hear it when I closed my eyes. That was over.

It was all over, now. There could be no more destruction, for I had nothing left to lose; and the one death that remained would be accepted with peace and resignation.

The wind was whistling in the chimney; and I suddenly felt cold. A spring chill, that was all that it was: but as I closed the window I began to cough.

# X 1861

# Philippa:

The cough started rather innocuously, actually, just a little here and there, nothing to cause any alarm. I was far from being upset by it; I was much more concerned with my life on the *Sea-Star*.

There were others coughing as well, that spring; and soon it seemed to have become an epidemic. My own had grown rather worse; I was occasionally spitting up phlegm now, which was more disturbing; but it was out of the question to see the ship's doctor, so I took deep breaths and told myself that it would pass.

By summertime we were going up and down the Brittany coast, precarious navigating at best; but we were all convinced that the *Sea-Star* was protected.

Not so her crew, however, for in June someone died of that same hacking cough. He was spitting up blood in the end;

and, by that time, many more of us had come down with it.

The captain ordered the doctor to examine all of us and find some medication.

It was night. I stood alone on the deck, shivering and afraid. The wind had started up again, kicking the waves into a white froth; the lighthouse which had been visible earlier in the evening had now vanished from sight. I could still detect a few lights glimmering from the shore, though. . . how far out were we? I couldn't tell.

The cough started again, then, and I doubled over until it passed. Oh, sweet gentle Jesus, am I doing what is right? It seems to be suicide — and suicide is a mortal sin. Yet it is my only chance. . . .

I took a deep breath, and dove into the water.

I knew that my first greatest danger was the _Sea-Star_ itself, that in order to be safe I had to get away from her side as quickly as possible. But the water was icy cold — horribly, painfully, impossibly cold. I came up gasping and choking, my muscles immobilized, my body weighing too much to remain afloat. . . .

But I had to. Survival. . . what was it that Yves had said about that, back in the sunshine of Saint Malo? About my mother? "She survived longer than many others do." A survivor, my mother: could I attempt anything less?

The icy water closed over my head again and this time I fought it. I surfaced quickly, kicking my legs, pulling with my arms, willing my body to obey, to survive.

God only knows how I did.

The _Sea-Star_ had disappeared into the night. I tried to orient myself, to find which direction I wanted, where those blinking lights lay — irony of ironies, if I were to inadvertently swim out to sea! And thank God, thank God that they had taught me to swim at all.

There. I caught a glimpse of a light — yes, there it was again. Come on, Philippa, I urged myself, you must survive. It was a prayer, a talisman, you must survive, you must survive. It was the only thing that remained between me and death, that kept me alive and afloat in those freezing waters. I will survive.

How many hours was I there? One, two? I lost all sense of time. My strength was sapped and all of my muscles ached — praise to the Lord that I had had this time to build them up! — only that ragged determination drove me onward. My breath was coming in shorter and shorter gasps now, and the cough was returning. . . . Oh, God, forgive me, I did not mean to kill myself. You know that.

I knew then that I was going to die and I was sad. There was so much to do, to see, to feel. . . and Yves, Yves who would feel responsible for my death. My God, I am truly sorry to have offended. . . .

When the sand came up under my feet I didn't even know what it was. And, after that, there was nothing but darkness.

# XI 1861

## Aurélie:

The dream had come again during the night, the one about the ship and the storm and the figure going overboard, and it disturbed me even more this time.

I woke early, just before dawn, and started breakfast. Mimi woke up then, too, and sat watching me with round eyes. "We'll take a walk down to the cove this morning," I told her cheerfully, and she laughed and jumped out of bed and danced all around me until I had to feed her to get her out of my way.

Something was not right. Something had happened during the night, but I wasn't quite sure what. There had been no storm, not really, just a little more wind than was usual. I dismissed the dream from my mind and started helping Mimi dress.

The sun was just coming up when we set out. I love that

magical morning time, when the world is fresh and damp and green and one feels as though one is the first ever to experience it. Mimi skipped ahead of me on the path, chanting some absurd rhyme in a singsong voice, and I didn't bother to hush her.

Then we were down on the sand and I saw him.

He was lying near the edge of the water and for a sudden cold moment I thought that he was dead. Mimi had stopped and hid behind my skirts, peering out around them curiously, her thumb in her mouth. I took a deep breath. Maman's voice was in my head, and I listened to her: "Trust your dreams. They are always there for a reason, to tell you something."

Slowly I walked down to where the still figure lay.

## XII 1861

# Philippa:

The world came back to me slowly and fuzzily, alarmingly out of focus. I opened my eyes and saw the sand on which I lay, but then it started tilting at a dizzying angle and I had to close them again.

Then I heard her voice.

It was a child's voice, innocent and curious. "Hello? Hello?" and I realized that I was going to have to open my eyes again. The prospect did nothing to delight me.

This time the sand wasn't tilting quite as much as before, and after a moment I began to cautiously test my muscles. They all seemed to be there — although the chorus of pain that they were setting up was unbelievable — and I gingerly raised my head. The crowd of people which swam for a moment before my eyes resolved itself to a woman, sitting very still on the sand and watching me, and a very small girl with eyes like saucers. I smiled and said something which sounded like a croak, and went back to sleep.

When I awoke they were still there. The woman was sitting a little closer to me than before, and the child was playing further down on the sand; but they were still there. I struggled to sit up.

"Be careful, monsieur," the woman said softly, "you are still very weak." I ignored her caution and drew myself up until I was at least relatively upright. Then I looked at her.

She was young; my age, perhaps, or a little older. She had long black hair, very thick and very straight, which she had tied back as though she couldn't be bothered with it. Her eyes were large and dark and there was something in them that I didn't quite know what to make of, some dreamy quality . . . she was not beautiful by most standards, her eyes were too large and her mouth too wide, and yet there was immediately an immense attraction.

I took a deep breath, which of course was a mistake, for it started me coughing again. She watched me, looking concerned, and when it was over I gasped, "It's — all right. I'm — much better." Still she said nothing, so I finally inquired, "Where am I?"

"Near Saint-Pol-des-Fougères."

On the south coast of Brittany, then . . . and all was apparently well, she accepted me as a man. Not that it mattered now.

"I fell overboard," I said, helpfully, into the silence.

Across her face was a flicker of — amusement? It couldn't be. And still she was silent, as was the little girl, who had by now approached and was standing by her. Her daughter? She looked too young. . . .

"My name is Philippe Chardonnais," I ventured at length; it seemed as though nothing could be accomplished with someone who refused to talk. Saint Pol — perhaps from here I could go on, to Nantes possibly, join up with another ship when my cough was gone. I would need help, and certainly shelter for some time. I looked at her speculatively.

"I am Aurélie Rousseau," she said, matching politeness with politeness. "My niece, Madeleine."

We looked at each other for a moment, and I could feel the bubbles of laughter rising. With all of my problems, I had to sit here and fence verbally with this woman. . . as I began to laugh, her eyes widened in surprise, but she joined in, and the frail morning sun shimmered all around us, and there was peace.

I started coughing then, and again she waited silently for it to pass, still with the air of concern making her eyes brighter, less dreamy. When it was over, she asked, "How long has it been like that?"

I shrugged. "I don't know. Since the winter, I suppose."

"You have done nothing about it, other than go swimming in cold water at night?" There was decidedly a glint of amusement there now. I saw that a response was not necessary, and silence descended again. She was watching me, waiting. I breathed deeply. It was now or never.

"Mademoiselle, perhaps you could tell me where I might lodge for a few days before setting off." I searched my pockets and came up with a few coins. "I have little money, as you see. But I would gladly work for the lodgings."

She spoke abruptly. "Keep your money; you will stay in my house. And do not call me mademoiselle, no one ever has done so. My name is Aurélie." She stood up. "We will go now. My house is on the cliffs, and you are very weak, so we should start at once."

She was right; we had to stop several times on the steep path because of my cough. I was feeling very weak — realizing what a miracle it was that I had survived at all.

The little girl, who Aurélie called Mimi, skipped and sang on the path ahead of us. I was a little concerned about her decision, once I saw the lonely isolated cottage. "What will the people of Saint Pol think? You must not live alone here with me. I should seek shelter elsewhere. . . ."

She indicated a chair, and I sat down gratefully: my legs were shaking from the climb. "It is of no consequence," she said, going to a cupboard, coming back with a vile-smelling liquid. "Here, drink this."

"What is it?"

"It will help you. It will clear out your chest."

It was, indeed, vile. She smiled as she watched me.

"You will take some of this every day, and sit in the sunshine, and soon there will be no more coughing. My mother taught it to me." She carefully capped the bottle. "The people of the village understand that I am not like them. You may stay here; there is no problem."

I looked at her curiously. She was not like any woman I had ever known — except perhaps the nuns: there was that same silent dignity, that sense of peace. "What do you mean, that you are not like them?"

"They are afraid of me. They tell stories about me to their children, to frighten them."

I laughed again, which was a mistake; it set off the coughing. Oh, Lord, just don't let her bring out that bottle again.

She waited until it had passed, then said, "You will see. They say that my mother was a witch, and that I am like her. If you live here, there are things that you must know. They leave me alone, except for a few who know me."

"Are you?"

She looked at me quickly, as if startled by my directness, but she didn't answer. Instead she called to Mimi, and the two of them prepared some soup which she watched me eat. There was fresh bread, too, and cheese, and wine; it was a feast, the first food I had tasted for too long. I ate ravenously.

Aurélie took up my bowl and pointed toward a ladder in the corner of the room. "There: you'll be sleeping in the loft. So up now."

"It couldn't be noon yet!" But my protest was half-hearted. Bed sounded wonderful.

"So? You are ill, you must sleep."

I stood up, swaying slightly, and barely made it upstairs before sleep overtook me. The bed was freshly made up, as if she had been expecting someone.

My head was reeling, light and dizzy and warm. I remember wondering where she had put the sleeping powder, in the soup or in the wine, and then the blackness came down.

## XIII <u>1861</u>

# Aurélie:

*O*nce the stranger started living in our house I could begin going up to the menhirs again, and for this I was grateful. I didn't want to take Mimi there, not yet, but she was so young and I didn't like leaving her alone in the house. So I left her with him, which delighted her, as she didn't have to do the lessons which I insisted upon. Instead, they would take walks, or play down at the cove; he made her dolls, too, out of wood. Mimi had never owned a doll before.

It was a long time before the menhirs began to speak to me again. Perhaps the god was angry that I had been away for so long — or perhaps it was I who did not listen, as I was full of thoughts of the foreigner.

He never said anything when I came back, never asked where I'd been; but I caught him looking at me with speculation once or twice in the firelight.

The garden was good to us that year. Summer had gone, but there was still much to be harvested, and he helped me with it. Sometimes I would see him working in the garden by himself — the men of Saint Pol never work in the gardens.

The village had been all agog for weeks after he came. As soon as he was strong enough, he went down every day to morning mass — the early one, which the priest said especially for the fishermen — and everyone watched him very closely. Marie was up at the house soon after his appearance, full of curiosity.

But soon, in their own way, they accepted him; and then no one stared any more.

He wasn't really handsome — not in the strong, virile way that Christophe and Antoine were — although I would have said that he was as strong as any of them. In his own way, though, he was beautiful, with fine, aristocratic features and eyes that were always laughing. He bought a razor in the village soon after he came, and left it out by the soap-dish, though I never saw him use it. He accepted, reluctantly, that I make him some clothes, but was very modest; even in the hot weather, he never took off his shirt as many of the other men did.

His learning amazed me. He was two years younger than I, and had been a mere cabin boy, yet he had read Plato and Sophocles and Aquinas and Descartes; he knew mathematics; he spoke fluent English. This I learned one day when Mimi came in and, giggling, said some nonsense. "Stop talking gibberish," I said automatically, not even turning away from the stove. She laughed, and said finally, "It's English, Aurélie!"

"English!" I was dumbfounded. "How did you learn it?"

"From Monsieur Philippe, of course"

He was very patient, very gentle with Mimi. When she was hurt, he could comfort her far better than I — I hated it when she whined or cried, but he would hold her and talk to her until the sobs subsided into faint hiccups; soon she would be laughing.

"I don't know how you do that with her."

"But, Aurélie, she's a child. Children cry."

"I don't like it when she does."

I had never seen Mimi so happy.

It was late September. By all rights, the winds should be starting; but it was an enchanted year, the thread of time spinning out golden and fine in the warm sunlight.

I always took Mimi with me when I went to do the laundry. All of the women of Saint Pol went to the same place, to the stream below the mill, where it was wide and the stones were large and flat, good for washing. We were in the middle of Saint Martin's summer, and it was hot: all of us pinned our hair up into loose chignons, rolled up our sleeves when we worked.

Marie was there, with her son Jean-Luc and her daughter Adèle; Mimi ran at once to play with them. Marie smiled when she saw me coming, and I put my basket down beside hers, kneeling on the flat rock, beginning to wash the clothes; there were more to do, now that the foreigner was with us.

"So, Aurélie, what is it like, having a foreigner living in your house?"

I shrugged. What did she want me to say?

"Monsieur *le curé* says that he is the most faithful communicant in the village, better even than old Madame Duroc."

"That I don't believe," I said, scrubbing at a vest. "She is always there, isn't she?"

"Ah, but she falls asleep during his homily on Sundays!" Marie laughed, her voice golden in the sunlight which reflected off the water. It was dappled sunlight, because of the trees; but golden and warm. Too warm: there were beads of perspiration on my forehead.

Marie's voice went on. "That's the greatest sin in Saint Pol, you know, falling asleep in church." She looked at me, a bright, quick glance. "What's he like, Aurélie?"

Again I shrugged. "What do you want? He's intelligent, and very kind, and good to both of us. He speaks English, and now Mimi is forever babbling in it. It sounds barbaric to me."

She laughed. "And what does he say to you?"

Oddly, I didn't like that question: it seemed an invasion of privacy, of what was mine. I liked my privacy; my aloofness from the village always safeguarded it for me. I carefully wrung out one of his tunics and didn't answer.

She was looking at the shirt. "He's not handsome, you know," she said, ignoring my rudeness: Marie was used to me by now. "But, in his own way — I don't know, there's something very attractive there."

I was leaning far over the water, rinsing. "Yes, I know."

"Do you love him, Aurélie?"

The question took me by surprise: I had never thought of it; I had never loved anybody but my mother. "Of course not!" My voice was too heated. "I do wish that you'd find something else to babble about, for a change! He's very kind, but that is all. Do you hear me?" I finally caught myself and lowered my voice. "Besides, he will be leaving soon."

"Will he?"

"Of course. He is much stronger now. It was good to have him with us, but soon he will go back to his own life and we will be as before."

She was off on another tangent. "It is said that he spends a great deal of time down by the boats in the harbor, asking many questions. Perhaps he would like to stay here."

I was surprised at the sharp feeling in my chest when she said that. "It's out of the question, Marie. How can you compare our little fishing boats to his great ships? It's an entirely different sort of life. Why would he want to stay in such a place, when he travels about all the time, from city to city? This is foolish talk."

I couldn't see her face as she bent forward. "Perhaps it is, Aurélie. But I was down at the harbor yesterday, with the children, and heard that Philippe Duroc is looking for men. He teased me about stealing Jean-Luc, if he were only a little older." I glanced at the three children, still deeply absorbed in their play. "If he were to stay here, perhaps there would be another wedding at the church, Aurélie."

I gathered the clothes in my basket and stood resolutely, balancing the basket on my hip as the women of Saint Pol do, pushing a few strands of damp hair away from my forehead. Marie sat back on her heels watching me, also arranging her hair with her hands, fixing a sleeve that had come unrolled.

"You and everyone here can only think of getting married, can't you? And I ask you, what good did it do my sister? I need no one, not even the foreigner. He is good and kind, but one day he will walk out of Saint Pol and never give any of us another thought, and Mimi and I will live on as we did before." There will be no more firelight talks, I thought, no lessons in the garden, no more new dolls for Mimi to play with. No more escapes, for me, up to the standing stones, no one to repair our roof when it leaks, no one to tease me about my seriousness and silence. No more discussions of philosophy. . . .

I had come into the kitchen one morning while the foreigner sat there with Mimi. There had been much wind during the night, and I was afraid, as always, for our frail shed. Mimi sat up eagerly, questioning.

"Is it all right?"

"Yes. The god has seen to his own." I had spoken without thinking.

The foreigner looked at me strangely. "What a pagan you are, Aurélie."

"I don't know what that means. I am Catholic to the god of the Catholics. . . ."

"But for you there is another."

How could I explain, to him, the voices and the standing stones and the visions? "There is one who gives me power. I don't know what it is called."

"Is that why they called your mother a witch? Because she had this power, too?"

"Partly. Maman could — see things, not the way other people do, but see them long before they happen, or long after. She knew — oh, so many things, how to cure maladies that the doctor wouldn't touch, and how to mix potions. . . and she could read your thoughts, sometimes, as well. It was frightening." I stopped, startled at how much I had said. Never had I spoken to anyone before of this, not even to Marie. I never ever talked about my mother.

"And now you have this power?"

"A little, not as much. I sometimes see things."

That bothered him; I could tell. He turned away then and talked to Mimi of other things.

Now, Marie looked at me, her eyes appraising. Sometimes I wondered at our friendship: there was so much between us — my visions were the least of all there was. What did she want me to say?

"Mimi, come on, we're going home." Then I turned to Marie. "I do not wish to marry the foreigner, even if he were to ask me. You and your tongue! I must go now."

And I went, but I could feel her eyes following me. Damn Marie, for making me think, think about what it would be like when the foreigner left. How sad and empty it would be. . . .

I was unnecessarily abrupt with him that evening, and the next day at dusk I went to the menhirs. The voices spoke; but, this time, I didn't want to listen. I covered my ears and screamed and wept; but it was to no avail.

It is well known that the gods are stronger than we are.

## XIV <u>1861</u>

# Philippa:

The days I spent with Aurélie and Mimi in the house on the headland stretched into weeks, and finally into months. It was nearly October, and still I stayed, finding one pretext after another. The roof needed repairing; Mimi was learning to speak English. I knew that they were not real reasons; but still I stayed.

Aurélie continued to surprise me. She had very little formal learning, but an intuitive knowledge which far surpassed anything that she could ever have found in a book. I realized nearly from the beginning that she was not concerned with the way people seemed, but looked inside, beyond, to see hearts and minds and souls. She was often abrupt, sometimes rude, but I could see that this was because of her rich interior life, her voices and visions; it must have been difficult for her to leave them for the wearisome everyday company of human beings.

I went down to the harbor sometimes, to look at the boats there, the fishing fleet. The people of Saint-Pol seemed to have accepted me at length — not as one of them, that would have been absurd — but as a welcome and honored visitor.

I found peace there, peace as I had never known it before. It was a hard life, I knew: long cold hours out at sea, for a catch that might or might not come; the sudden storms which seemed to appear out of nowhere on this part of the coast, dashing fishing boats against the hard murderous rocks and reefs as if they were nothing but dry tinder.

But there was the other side of it, too, the one I was beginning to see, that which had been denied me on the *Sea-Star:* coming home at night, cold and stiff and sore, to a warming fire, a hot meal, the warmth of another person. Relaxing over a cup of cider; watching the old men play *pétanque* on the square in front of the church. Mass on Sundays, with the church crowded; weekday Mass, quiet and intimate — I felt myself growing closer to God than ever before at the convent. Room to live; room to breathe; a patch of soil to call one's own — that was how life was meant to be.

Aurélie was amazed. "Why, you come from a grand city, and still you like it here? We have nothing!"

"Here," I told her seriously, "you have everything."

She taught me, Aurélie, things that I would never have dreamed of. One night, sitting by the fire, Mimi quite asleep, she handed me a cup filled wtih some hot steaming liquid. "Here, drink this."

"What is it, another of your vile medicines?"

"Why must you be forever arguing with me? Drink it."

The world was reeling and spinning about me: there were colors flashing. Then, suddenly, everything steadied; but I was no longer at the cottage on the headland, I was back at the convent, watching a procession of nuns gathering around a bed. I tried to see who was lying there, but I couldn't. There was a priest there, too, and with a shock I realized that he was administering the last rites. But for whom?

The nuns were singing, their voices rising and falling, the candles that they held in their hands flickering. I looked for some I might know: there was Mother Superior, looking grave and recollected; Mother Julian knelt near her. Others were grouped about: nuns who had taught me, cared for me, loved me.

There was incense there, too, wisping about the black-shrouded figures. What a beautiful way to die, surrounded by singing and prayers and candlelight; it seemed like a foretaste of heaven.

Then someone moved and I saw who was on the bed. It was Sister Natalie.

Someone was shaking me gently, and I gasped as cold water was splashed on my cheeks. Everything was fuzzy for a moment, and then the world steadied itself and I saw Aurélie standing over me, Aurélie concerned and biting her lip in concentration. She had a glass of water in her hand.

"What is it? What happened?"

"You are all right." Her voice, as always, was calm. "Just rest now."

I struggled up on my elbows. The fire was still blazing merrily, and I tried to look at the clock on the mantelpiece, but my eyes wouldn't focus. "What happened?"

"I think that it was not so pleasant, the place where you went." She sat down beside me, still holding the glass. "I am sorry. The first time should be better than that."

"But what happened?"

"You drank a tea that I make; it makes the visions more clear. Things that have something to do with your life." She looked at me curiously. "Was it so very bad, what you saw?"

I shrugged. I was beginning to recover now. She had

opened a window for me into her world, and I was not at all sure that I liked what I saw of it.

We laughed a great deal together, Aurélie and I, and it was with a start that I realized that I had never had a close friend before. Isabelle and I had been friends at school, but that was because of shared experiences: we were both in the same place and making the best of it. I envied Aurélie her friendship with Marie, but knew that I couldn't join in it: I was the foreigner, a man, who cannot share women's talk. Once or twice I thought of telling her the truth about myself, but thought better of it. Lies are hard to admit to.

We taught each other things, too, during that short time together. We would walk in the woods, and she would name roots and plants for me, telling me how they could be used. We would sit late by the fire, poring over an ancient book she had full of flowers and plants, their names inscribed below the pictures in spindly writing; it had been her mother's. "That is hemlock," she said, pointing. "It is poison; it—"

"I know. That's how Socrates was executed; he drank hemlock."

Her eyes were wide. "Who is Socrates?" And we would sit up longer so that I could tell her of Socrates and ancient Greece.

One evening, though, I saw our life together from a different perspective; and then I knew that it was time to leave.

Supper was simmering. I was outside with Mimi, playing with one of her dolls, her laughter warm in the twilight. Aurélie came to the door to call us, and stayed in the doorway watching, a half-smile on her face. Mimi ran on in, and I followed; but I too stopped in the doorway for a moment.

It was dusk, and as she turned her head to face me, there was a line running down the center of her face dividing her features so that half were in light and half in shadow. Her hair, tied into a single braid, fell down the front of her shoulder; I remember very clearly the stains on her apron.

I don't know how long we stood there like that, looking at each other, only a few inches of air separating us; it seemed an eternity. She caught her breath suddenly, biting her lower lip, looking for all the world like Mimi when she had done something wrong; my heart was hammering in my chest. Oh, God, Blessed Mother of God, it has happened, the impossible has happened.

The moment was gone then, and we turned and went into the room; supper, bright conversation followed. But all the while I felt a piece of lead in my stomach.

I am a woman, Philippa Chardonnais, seventeen years old. I pretended to be a boy for a while, it is true, but only so that I could do as I wished with my life; if women could go to sea, I should never have masqueraded as something I was not.

Yet I had, and now I was reaping a bitter harvest.

For I was in love with Aurélie Rousseau.

She liked me, I knew. I was a younger brother to her, perhaps, a companion certainly for those long lonely evenings on the clifftop. But — even if she, too, loved me, as I thought I had seen in that still moment in the doorway — then what? She loved Philippe Chardonnais, the cabin boy; she never dreamed I was deceiving her. If she had, she would surely hate me.

There was only one response. I could not go on here, loving her as I did: it was wrong. For all of us.

There was only one thing to do, and I did it. Long before the morning mists had left the fields, long before the standing stones began to whisper to her dreams, long before even the priest or the fishermen were about, I left.

# *Mimi:*

*A*dèle and I thought of each other as sisters for most of our lives. It was that way: we played together, while Aurélie and Marie washed clothes or took us to school or waited for the fishing boats to return. There was never any mystery about Adèle: we didn't need to go through the nonsense and struggles that Aurélie and Philippa had. We knew from the start that we loved each other, and it was simple, and good. Never questioned, never challenged.

I know that they had questions, especially Philippa. She had been raised by nuns, after all: their strict morality, their rigid judgments were stamped upon her. She relaxed with time, though, rejoicing in her life, in the love that they had, for each other and for me.

I was their daughter. After they made the decision to be married, to live together as a couple, no one questioning Phi-

lippa's male identity, they wanted to adopt me. I alone refused: I had my name, I said, and I would keep it. They never
pressed me about it; and I was, truly, their daughter in every
other way.

There were hard times at the beginning for them, of
course. Philippa had left once she realized that she was in love
with Aurélie; and Aurélie was miserable with her gone. I never
knew quite what was happening — I was still very young; but
I do remember the strong sense of loneliness which pervaded
the house, the melancholy. Aurélie had that side to her, a part
of her that belonged to the grey mists and the bleak twilights
of depression, fine rain and murky light. And once Philippa
had left, she abandoned herself to it.

## XVI <u>1861-1862</u>

# *Aurélie:*

*C*he days after the foreigner left were grey, all of them; it was as if the sun was something remembered from a happier past, a memento to be cherished, something to think about on the long winter nights when the wind howled outside and the waves whipped the shoreline with the fury of all the gods.

He had left before I could tell him that I knew his secret.

I had not seen it up by the menhirs, of course. It was not clear — not like the images I had had of my mother's dying, or anything like that; just a taste of salt and the sound of horses' hooves on cobbled streets; just a glimpse of women in long black gowns, and a little girl with Philippe's eyes playing in a walled courtyard. I saw that, and many others like it, in those quiet days of Saint Martin's summer, while Mimi learned English and the foreigner learned how to behave like a man; but I said nothing, I didn't want to break the holding spell. The days spun out, shimmering silk in the golden liquid sunlight which dappled the standing stones; I knew that the gods have their own time, and it was their spell, not mine.

And then she left on a grey rainy dawn, and I lay awake listening to her go, the tears running silent and useless down to wet my pillow. I never even noticed at what point I changed the pronoun when I thought of her.

As I had told Marie it would happen, life did go on as usual. Autumn came in earnest, a chill wind whistling around the house on the headland, a chill creeping into one's bones as one went about one's business. I had begun to do some sewing, and now walked down the path to the village nearly every day with Mimi, me for the work, and Mimi for lessons at the rectory.

It was as well that I had that kind of contact with people, because I was so close to depression. I could sit for hours in the cottage or up by the menhirs, not opening myself to visions or voices, simply staring into space until, with a start, I remembered where I was. All that I could think of was the foreigner, the evenings together, the times I had longed to reach out and touch her, caress her hair, whisper in her ear. I wondered sometimes, if I had done so, if she would have stayed; I thought perhaps so. And so I blamed myself for her going.

Marie must have seen the darkness descending on me, for she was gentle and careful with me. She invited me to her house for many different reasons, and I went obediently, silent and unresponsive to her overtures of friendship. "You miss him so much, then, Aurélie."

"Yes."

Winter followed autumn, and it was that winter that Mimi began to have visions. Perhaps our isolation fostered them; perhaps her daily communion with the elements on the lonely headland made more sense to her than the muttered Latin phrases at church; I didn't know. But she told me her dreams, dreams filled with futures and questions, and I knew that soon I would have to take her up to the standing stones.

She was irritating, too, with the foreigner gone. She had fulfilled such a great role in Mimi's life: the father she did not have, the mother I could never be. Mimi expected that kind of attention to continue, and I was incapable of giving it to her. Sometimes she would go to Marie's house for the day, and Marie would mother her, and Jean-Luc and Adèle would play with her, and things would get better for a while. But she asked about the foreigner, incessant questions, and I had no answers.

Worst of all, the menhirs were silent.

No voices; no visions; no whispers. All was gone, lost when the foreigner left.

I knew what it was like to be alone, of course. I had been alone, one way or another, for all of my life, yet never had been lonely. I had never required the presence of another human being; people were a nuisance, intruders on my private world, invaders of my space who were to be endured, not welcomed.

My mother and I had lived in the same rooms, breathed the same air, yet had lived in different worlds: it never occurred to me to miss her, to feel anything but a melancholic regret at her death.

And now I was aching because the foreigner was gone.

I found the hours in a day to be long and tedious and empty. I picked up one task, only to put it down again, and then to pick it up later for want of anything else to do. Mimi followed me about, whining and complaining.

And still the standing stones were silent.

I still went to them daily, of course. They were my only comfort, the thread which held my life together. I went, and cried, and listened: but all that came back to me was the echo of my own grief. Perhaps the god was gone; perhaps, too, I was meant to learn something within my solitude. Knowledge acquired too easily is no gift.

Aloneness I cherished, but her absence was unbearable. A subtle distinction, yet one of infinite importance.

## XVII <u>1861-1862</u>

## *Philippa:*

The convent was essentially in the heart of the city, yet separated from it by high stone walls and imposing wrought-iron gates. Anyone seeking to enter for any reason had to first ring a bell, at which signal Sister Portress would come out, clutching her shawl about her shoulders, and inquire as to one's business.

One entered into a small dirt courtyard. The school was directly ahead, imposing stone with ivy creeping up its sides, the impressive front entrance and the smaller one which we as students had always used, which led to a long glistening hallway where morning prayers were said below the statue of Our Lady.

Beyond, to the right, was the chapel, at the center of the compound, with a huge fir tree in front of it, shading the entrance. Behind the chapel, with its rows of stalls and benches for the nuns and ranks of chairs for the students, was the convent itself. Beyond that were the terraces and the garden, running down a gentle slope towards the sea, until stopping at the impregnable outer wall, which ran all around the compound like the ramparts of some medieval castle, protecting the inhabitants from the evils of the world beyond.

The bells of the chapel governed the time spent within those walls. They rang the hours of the day, of course; but far more important were the other hours, those announcing the Masses, the times for prayer — different bells summoning sisters and students to the chapel. The sisters had the Daily Office to say; but there were many other bells and times for prayer as well.

I knew the school by heart, through long association; I knew the long winding stone staircase sweeping up to the upper levels; I knew the flagstones in the kitchen, the plants and etchings which adorned the students' refectory. I knew the dormitories, the classrooms, the offices. The school had long been my home.

Now I was discovering the cloister.

I was a postulant, lowest of the low, confined to the novitiate to all intents and purposes, yet subtly in a different place from the school which I had left such a short time ago. A short time... only a lifetime away.

The sisters were Franciscans, vowed to missionary work, so those at the school — which was also the Motherhouse — were either very old, having retired as it were from the taxing duties they had undertaken in remote corners of the world; or else very young, novices and the newly-professed, still learning the ways of the cloister.

It was, I told myself firmly, what I wanted. To stay here, and bind myself firmly to God, and to God alone: and then to be sent far away, to India or Ceylon or Scandinavia, to a new world requiring all of my concentration. That would keep her away from my thoughts, I whispered fiercely to myself: that would keep her away. It was the best that I could pray for.

The novitiate, when I joined it, was large: fifteen juniors, who had made their first vows; eight novices, still "on trial," as it were, for one year; and two others like myself, clad in simple black skirts and blouses, postulants, not far advanced enough to even be called "Sister."

There was one other, of course; but she was only there in my mind. Sister Natalie, whose death I had seen from so far away, and who I had so admired; Natalie walked the cloisters with me, prayed with me, ate with me. I thought of her, fiercely, to keep myself from thinking of Aurélie.

I recognized many of the novices and juniors from my years at the school; unlike me, they had gone directly from graduation into postulancy. Perhaps, for them, the call had been immediate and clear.

My own vocation I questioned. I had run away from Aurélie, that much was obvious; and yet, now that I was here, all of the old feelings returned: the devotions, the pure joy of the chanting and the ecstasy which swept me up and carried me forward. Time passed, as it does in a convent, somehow differently from in the world; six months after leaving Saint-Pol-des-Fougères, I was clothed as a novice and given as my name in religion the title Sister Mariette. To all intents and purposes, I belonged.

"For your penance, you will recite the seven penitential psalms at the foot of the crucifix in the garden." The voice seemed to come from very far away, as I sat quietly in one the long rows of black and white nuns. The sister who had received this penance rose from her knees, bowed, and silently took her place again as the next one went forward.

"I accuse myself of having missed an Office through laziness." Her voice was subdued. The woman on the chair before her nodded slightly, then said, "For your penance you will beg for your soup in the refectory this evening."

The young sister rose, bowed, and walked back to the seat, and I stifled a yawn. How tedious, how incredibly tedious this entire procedure was!

Sister Clara, the Novice Mistress, said that I couldn't yet appreciate all of the aspects of community life; and she must be right. "Although you caught a glimpse of cloistered life during your time here as a student, you could neither comprehend nor appreciate all of our practices." Her eyes shone behind her spectacles; it was very clear that Sister Clara was glad that one of the stray lambs had returned to the fold.

"I am so glad," she had told me warmly on that first rainy morning when I knocked on the convent door, "so glad, dear child, that after exploring the world you have come to the conclusion that there is no better life than one spent serving Our Lord. Welcome home, my dear."

That had been a long time ago; it was now almost April. And I was, truly, willing to try. I forced myself to conform to the ways of an obedient religious: I read all of the books that they gave me — St. Thomas Aquinas and St. Benedict and St. Augustine; I was prompt at prayers, and put all of my soul into meaning every word of them. I worked in the kitchen and in the garden and in the school; I listened to the Novice Mistress' addresses to the novitiate, did penance for my faults, scrubbed floors and studied theology. I did everything that I possibly could.

If I had been a different person, perhaps it might even have worked.

It took me a long while to realize that one does not need to wear the habit of a Sister in order to serve God.

It took me a long time to realize that having a family and living a good life is equally acceptable to God.

And it took me longest of all to realize that, somehow, Aurélie and Mimi and I could constitute such a family.

The question, of course, was: what of Aurélie? What

would she say when — if — I returned to the house on the cliffs and told her that I loved her? What would she say when she realized that I was a woman?

Over and over in my mind I rehearsed the scene. I lay awake at night on my narrow cot, seeing her face, hearing her laughter, wanting with all of my being to hold her and be with her, to laugh and talk and play and learn and grow together with her.

As the lilacs appeared in the convent garden, as the light of day prolonged itself into the evening, I realized that I could no longer live a lie, that I would have to leave the convent soon. That, whatever her response was to me, I should have to see her again.

And, one morning in May, I thanked the sisters, told them I had a mistaken vocation, that I wanted to marry, after all, and walked out of the convent for the last time.

## XVIII 1897

# Mimi:

If I have anything to reproach Aurélie and Philippa with, it would be for giving me such a happy childhood. I never suspected that things might not be always happy and golden and glorious as they were in those days; I wasn't told that there was a darker side to life.

They were married soon after Philippa returned from Saint Malo. She continued to pretend, for everybody but us, that she was a man — I do not blame them for that, they could see no other way. Somehow, I never thought of it as being particularly odd.

I hadn't been officially told right away, of course. I don't think that they quite knew how to go about doing it. Philippa returned early one morning, wearing trousers and with a canvas bag slung over one shoulder; and I was sent away for a time, with hugs and assurances that she would still be there when I came back. I trotted happily down the path to the village, excited to be the one to tell Adèle and Jean-Luc and everybody else that the foreigner had returned to Saint Pol.

I don't think that they told me about Philippa for two or three years after that. I probably wouldn't have understood, if they had any sooner; as it was, it seemed to me to be a great fuss about nothing at all. In my mind, we had become a family the morning that Philippa had walked back into our lives and told us that she was staying.

Philippa started working one of the fishing boats, and Aurélie and Marie and Adèle and I took long walks over the headland, waiting for the boats to come back. Aurélie got to be very close to Marie in those times, for Philippa and Jacques, Marie's husband, were both on Yves Blériot's trawler. They waited together, talked together, laughed together, worried together. And, when it finally came in, they ran down to the harbor to meet it together.

They were good years, those times. Twelve of them, twelve years of calm and happiness and peace. Twelve years of having parents who cared deeply for each other and cared deeply for me.

Adèle and Jean-Luc and I went to the village school together, learning together all the things that our parents had learned. I expect that people might have suspected that Jean-Luc and I would eventually marry, but he died when he was nine years old, of a mysterious fever that swept through the village like wildfire. After that, Adèle and I were closer than ever; we pricked our fingers to draw blood and swore solemnly to always love each other, until death did us part. We kept the vow.

It was a grand affair, Aurélie and Philippa's wedding. A village such as Saint Pol treasures its moments of joy, of gaiety, for they are so few and far between; weddings and christenings are always important occasions. This wedding insured another hand on a fishing boat, a parent for a fatherless child

— me — and, perhaps most importantly for the village, it meant that the wild woman from the headland was a little less wild, a little more encompassed in the daily life of Saint Pol.

I remember so very little of it — I was allowed to sample the wine, which put me to sleep right away. It was probably no accident, that; for this was the first time that Aurélie and Philippa shared the same bed, and they hardly needed an inquisitive child about.

I learned of love from them — not just of love between two women, but of love between two people. They did not force me to do as they did; perhaps, had Adèle not already been in my life, I would have loved and married a young man from the village; I do not know. But, knowing their love as I did, their support and reassurance for each other, I found it natural to love Adèle as I did. After they died, and she came to live on the headland with me, people in the village thought nothing of it: companionship, they assumed, nothing more. And we lived there together until Adèle, too, had the fever that had killed her brother, and it killed her, too.

I wait alone on the headland now. I walk the sand of the cove alone now. They were my people, and now they are gone, all of them: nothing but hatred remains. Yet I feel rooted to this place — I cannot go, I know no other world.

And yet, when they were all here, how very happy I was. . . .

## XIX 1862

# Aurélie:

*I* was waiting for her when she returned.

I cannot say that it was a vision, for I saw nothing. There were no voices, no images of figures diving from ships at sea, no pictures of women in black; there was nothing. And yet, that morning when I arose, I knew that she would return then, and I spent the morning alternately bustling about in great activity, or standing still on the cliffs, waiting.

I sent Mimi down to Marie's house for the day, wanting our first moments together to be spent alone; I tied ribbons in my hair, laughing at myself for my foolishness, but doing it anyway. Every noise made me start. And finally, when I knew that it was time, I walked sedately down the path to the cove where we had first met.

She was sitting in the sand, her arms around her knees, watching the ocean.

I went and sat silently beside her, and she did not even look at me: she had known that I would come. There was a moment of silence then — not hard, taut silence, but silence that is soft and warm and comfortable and assuming. When she spoke, she was still watching the waves.

"My name is Philippa. My father was an English sailor who never knew that he had a child. My mother was a prostitute who was killed in a fight. I was raised in a convent in Saint Malo, and I had to leave it twice in order to find out where I really belong." She took a deep breath. "I love you. I think that I have loved you since the first time that I saw you and Mimi here. I want to live here with you, marry you, spend the rest of my life with you."

She stopped. I could only imagine what strength it had taken her to make that speech, what force had driven her back here: my kinds of visions have little to do with love. I reached for her hand.

"I know."

There was a sharp intake of breath, and she turned to me, tears running down her face. I wondered how long she had been crying like that. "You know. Of course you know. Did you, before I left?"

"Yes."

"Why did you say nothing?"

I shrugged. "It had to be your time, not mine. You had to struggle; I didn't."

"Can it work, then?"

I smiled. "We can make it work — Philippa."

## XX *1864*

# *Philippa:*

*C*here were roses in the garden the second year.

Aurélie didn't think much of them — flowers were frivolous, a luxury, without any real meaning; but I loved them. My utilitarian convent past, I suppose.... I revelled in touching them — the delicate, fragile petals that bruised so easily, the sharp thorns which were quick to draw blood: all of my senses were engaged in admiring those flowers. I tried to explain this to Aurélie one night after Mimi was asleep, when we sat up drinking cider and watching the fire and listening to the wind howl outside the house: there is nothing like a stormy night to make one feel snug and secure indoors. She heard me out patiently.

"Why are you so very fascinated with something which is painful?"

"It's not just the pain," I explained. "It's the contrast

between the flower and the thorns — between beauty and danger."

She was silent, and I began to wonder whether she was finding me too whimsical. Even now, with the wedding behind us and everything settled and secure, I still wondered if I was what she wanted, if she might not someday simply slip up to the menhirs and vanish in the mist.

She looked at me then, and smiled. "Like us, isn't it, Philippa?" she asked softly. "It's beautiful, but sometimes there's pain, as well."

Without thinking first, I spoke. "And the danger?"

She wouldn't look at me. "That too, Philippa."

Mimi had started school.

I think that it was the most difficult time for me, her beginning school, strange as that might sound. Mimi herself was glad — her friends all lived in the village, the children she played with, and she hadn't seen them often: now they were together every day at lessons.

Aurélie, I know, was relieved: she loved Mimi, but she had never really wanted the responsibility of being a mother and was glad to have those hours alone, hours she could spend with her soul and her silences, up by the standing stones.

So I alone worried. Out on the ocean, with the sea calm and the nets down, we sat in the sun and joked and passed the bread and salami, and I thought about her walking alone down the path and going through the village every day. I thought about terrible things, about her slipping on the rocks and falling off the cliff, and I felt fear. And too I thought about her laughing and playing with the other children, and how very much she needed their company. And, sometimes, I wondered about the time when we would have to tell her who I was.

They joked with me about it, the men on the fishing boat. "I remember how my Caroline worried when the little ones left — you remind me of her, my boy, just like a mother hen!"

and, "Aurélie must be *beside* herself, if the father fears so much!"

I forgot at what point they stopped remembering that I was not Mimi's father. I forgot when I started thinking of her as my child.

They came home late and started drinking Calvados until later still, sitting under the bright café awning and watching the harbor. They told stories of fish, and storms, and mermaid legends. The lighthouse out on the point blinked its regular warning — the lighthouse to which I owed my life, God using it as a beacon to guide me to shore that long-ago night — and time flowed by.

I rarely sat with them. The headland was there, waiting, and Aurélie with it. Aurélie and her wonderful soups, Aurélie and her strange visions, Aurélie laughing or arguing or silent — but still with that grave mystical undercurrent which made her who she was. I far preferred to spend my time with her; so I would stop at the church as I went through the village, stop to give thanks for safety and bounty, to ask for continued good weather and good catches — and then I would go up to the headland, to Aurélie.

It took me a very long time to discover that quarrels did not destroy the closeness, that there could be intimacy in conflict. The nuns who had raised me had taught me never to argue.

"I didn't ask you to live here so that you could change my life!" Her voice was heated, angry, and I instinctively withdrew: it was the first argument we had had. She didn't like my lack of response, either, and went on:

"You're gone all day — all *day* — out on that rotten ghastly boat of yours, and you come home and expect me to drop whatever I'm doing, even if it's important to me, to listen to all of your stories. Sometimes I don't *want* to listen to your stories, Philippa!"

"How do I know what you want to listen to? You're silent so much of the time, I can't ever tell what you're thinking. . . ."

"Then learn to hear the silence! Didn't that convent teach you anything about silence? I'm talking to you, all the time, in my silence!"

I felt fear when we argued, because I didn't know what the arguments meant — I didn't know what was being said beneath the words. After we argued, Aurélie always ran away — no matter what the weather or the time, she was gone: out into the night, with the wind whipping about her and her eyes filled with tears, running and stumbling on the path, searching for the shelter and the solace of the mists. I sat numbly, listening to the sound of the violent words echoing through the house in which they had been spoken — or shouted — and felt the tears coming, hot and sudden and unbidden.

I worried, too, about her alone. I worried about her anger, and her hurt, and how they would blind her to the elements; I would see her, too, falling off of the cliff and lying dead and unseen on the rocks below. I should have known, then, that Aurélie was in no danger, that she knew the elements better than most people know themselves, and that she would be safe.

I should have known then that she would never go off that cliff unless she meant to.

But time did flow on, and as it did I realized that there was trust in the anger, and that the warm undercurrent of love beneath supported and held the anger. It is a slow process, that of two people adapting the rhythms of their lives to each other: not becoming each other, or even part of each other — Aurélie and I could never do that, we were too much ourselves — but adapting to being with each other. I knew that there was intimacy even in pain, and that needing each other and giving to each other made the occasional hurt necessary — and bearable.

I had begun to read again. Books were expensive, and hard to come by; but I found that I needed them (how I missed the convent library in Saint Malo!), and the village priest had an address where one could write and have books sent to one through the mail... I was delighted. I bought as many as I could afford, sometimes two or three a month, and read them in a matter of evenings.

Aurélie was fascinated. "How can you do this? There is sunshine outside, and clouds, and the sand and the ocean! How much more do you need to know? What is it that they cannot teach you?"

I read mostly spiritual books at first, books that the priest recommended, books about the Sacred Heart and about saints and martyrs of long ago. Then I became interested in re-discovering literature from my school days, and went back to Racine and Corneille and Rabelais, finding so much more meaning in them than they had ever held for me in class. Aurélie chose to ignore it all; but Mimi was just learning to read then, herself, and the two of us would quite happily spend long hours together, her puzzling out the pronunciation of some word while I read on avidly. Sometimes, on a Sunday afternoon, we'd go down to the cove together, Mimi and I, and read and read and get terribly sunburned. Aurélie would just shake her head when we got home.

Until I sent for the volume of poetry.

I didn't send for it, not precisely: I had already bought a prerequisite number of volumes, and, as an incentive to continue buying, the booksellers had sent me a free book of their choice: it was poetry. I cannot remember who wrote it, for verse is something I have never enjoyed: I cannot think in rhymes. I left it on the kitchen table when it came and went out to work in the garden. When I came back later, it was gone.

I assumed, of course, that Mimi had taken it; and I thought no more of the entire affair. Until Aurélie began tak-

ing paper and ink with her on her long walks up the headland
to the standing stones.

I thought that perhaps she was painting; she had done
some in the past, before her mother died, then had decided
that she had no talent for such a thing and stopped. But she
took no colors with her, just the ink; and when I asked about
it she denied doing anything at all, so I left it at that.

Aurélie never told anybody anything until she was ready.
Not even me. Especially not me.

# XXI <u>1866</u>

## *Aurélie:*

*I*t would never have occurred to me not to marry Philippa: we loved each other, I wanted her to stay with me on the headland, to hold me and teach me things and be my friend; but sometimes life was more difficult together than I had anticipated. Philippa never seemed quite sure whether she was a man or a woman — oh, I cannot blame her for that, it was a precarious and difficult position that she was in, living two different lives; but it made me uneasy nonetheless. She listened to the men at work talking about their relationships with their wives, and she came back to the headland, expecting the same from me. But I never wanted to be anybody's wife: I married her so that we could live together in peace, that was all. I wasn't going to change who I was.

It was difficult for both of us, I think. Philippa had to learn so much — about me, about Mimi, about her work —

and, too, she was still considered a foreigner by the village. A loved and accepted one, to be sure; but a foreigner all the same. That must have hurt her deeply.

But I wasn't accustomed to thinking about other people so much, and it wearied me. I thought about Mimi — although, to be fair, she was less of a problem once Philippa came and the responsibility of her upbringing was shared — and I thought about Philippa, when I didn't want to be thinking about people at all.

I would go up to the standing stones and listen for the voices, but there were others now which competed with them: Philippa's voice, Mimi's voice, sometimes even Marie's voice — Marie was the only one from the village who dared to come into the cottage, who was not afraid that my mother may have cursed it; and she was often there. She told people that we were friends, and I suppose that we were, as much as I could be friends with anybody. I didn't want friends, not particularly — my world was complete in and of itself, stretching it to accommodate Philippa was already a trying task — but Marie seemed to expect it of me.

Since the wedding, the people in the village had become more friendly with me. It was as though that was the magic event, the moment which transformed me from the strange wild woman whose mother was a witch and who lived in an isolated clifftop cottage into a respectable normal lady. I didn't like that much; indeed, I didn't particularly wish to be a normal respectable lady — they seemed to have nothing in common with me — but the village was content, so I left it at that.

If they had known the truth, they would probably have killed us.

I don't say that lightly: I didn't know just what it was that we were doing, but I knew that it certainly wasn't done much, and never in Saint-Pol-des-Fougères. And my people... we are suspicious, I know that. There is a certain way of doing things, a way that things have been done in one's family for generations — and that is taken very seriously. It is not written down anywhere, it is never spoken of; but it is engraved on the hearts of the people. Any breach of tradition threatens the life of the village: how can one know that things will go on as they have done, if things suddenly change? I understand this.

And I knew that two women marrying each other was certainly a breach of tradition.

I know that Philippa feared discovery. She talked about it; she wanted us to plan for the day when we would tell Mimi, how we would explain to her the need for silence and secrecy. I worried less — but I saw less of the village than she did, it was not an immediate concern. Up by the standing stones, it was easy to forget.

I had other things on my mind. I was frightened that I might lose the voices, that domestic issues would cloud my mind and keep me away from those things in my life which gave me strength and nourishment. Philippa had begun reading books again, and I envied her: I never spoke of them, but I was jealous — jealous, not of her time away from me, but of the satisfaction she got from reading. She would look up from her book and her face would be glowing, alive, warm — the way that I used to feel when I returned from the menhirs. I ignored it, and never told Philippa of my feelings — mostly because I was ashamed to admit that I was frightened of losing the voices, my hold on the other world — but I would look away whenever the books were brought out. I would look at them sitting smugly in the little bookcase that she had built, and would go up to the standing stones and cry and cry.

Until the day that I found the poetry.

It was sitting on the kitchen table, a slim volume bound in red leather and embossed in gold. I don't know if she left it there for me on purpose — how could she have known that the words were already there, in my soul, without a means of expression? One would have to have been my mother in order to know that. . . .

I began to read, slowly — I hadn't read anything in years — and the rhythm of the verses caught me in its music, spinning out the words, making them soft and velvety and harsh and loud. . . soothing and compelling, like the rhythms of the sea below the cliffs. How many nights in my life had I lain awake listening to those rhythms? And here they were, written in a book by a person I would never know, who had been caught up, as I had, in the mysteries of the sea and of the earth, the music of the stars and the whispers of the wind! The words themselves held little attraction for me; they blended with the whole, rather than *being* the whole — it was an experience, and an event, and I was overwhelmed.

I took the book with me that day when I went to the standing stones. I stood and read the verses aloud, and the seasounds behind me became part of me, and the earth sighed, and the voices whispered. The mists came up and wrapped themselves about me and held me, their moistness touching my cheeks and hands with coolness, and still I read the poems.

I stopped when it was finally too dark to see the page.

The voices were there, whispering, comforting, accepting. I stood absolutely still, the book clasped against my breast, listening and breathing and feeling. And waiting.

When the vision came, and it was of my mother, I was not surprised.

I saw her alone, and young: younger than I was, walking the headland path. She had stopped and was kneeling down beside a tree, taking something from the bushes. . . and then she was walking again up the path, briskly, purposefully. She didn't look about her, but was smiling and humming softly to herself — I didn't recognize the tune, perhaps some popular air from the time when she was a girl. . . she had made her way through the brambles — no wonder I had found no path, she went forward as would a ghost, softly and delicately, and the branches closed again behind her as she went.

I was not surprised when she reached the standing stones and I saw for the first time what she held: paper, and a quill pen, and a bottle of ink.

She worked quietly for some time, writing and writing, stopping from time to time to close her eyes and breathe the air of the place — much as I was accustomed to do: my gestures were all hers. And then she rose, and read the words aloud, and I heard the same rhythms that I had discovered in the book. That was what poetry was, then: these words that caught at one's soul, that trapped one's heart into admitting that which it had already known: that the rhythms are within each of us, and that they are the same. I had never before felt linked to other human beings: but that night, standing in the clearing with the moon rising at my back and the dream-dust of the vision still sparkling about me, I began to understand. We were all the same, bound by the rhythms of our lives — all of us: my mother, and Chantale, and Christophe, and Mimi and Philippa and Marie... we all carried the words of the earth written at the center of our beings. That night, I began to feel.

A week later I began to write.

I had been shattered by my discovery, and had hidden the book in a cupboard, taking it out again and again when I was alone. But the ache was still there, the ache of words unspoken and tears unshed, and I trembled with all that was inside of me.

Philippa, I know, wondered about me. My silences grew, as I struggled to learn what would come of my discovery; and I know that my silences hurt her: she never did understand them very well.

"What are you doing? Do you pray?"

"Pray? You know better than that. I don't need to pray."

"That's what I do in my silences."

"That's the Christian way, Philippa. I don't think that you would call me a Christian, would you?"

And she was more perplexed than ever. But I understood even less than she. At a time when I had never felt more linked to other people, I was withdrawing more into myself.

I didn't know then that one cannot understand others until one understands oneself.

I began to write the next day.

It wasn't as difficult as I might have thought. Just as I had seen in my vision, I went to the stones with the paper, and sat and began to write. The words flowed from my mind to the paper, as freely as if I had nothing to do with their creation. Perhaps the voices were speaking in my soul; perhaps the words had been there, all along, waiting in the quiet dark recesses of my mind for the chance to free themselves. I don't know. I didn't question the process, I just let it happen: and the words came. I worked and worked, and sat and dreamed, and when at length I went back to the house on the headlands I too was glowing and alive and refreshed.

And, as though the words had liberated me, I could at last talk. I chattered to Mimi as we fixed supper, and played word games with both of them by the fireside, the love around us warm and strong. Philippa was watching me with wonder, Mimi with great excitement, and I laughed and laughed and laughed.

## XXII 1867

# Philippa:

Paradoxical as it may seem, it was Aurélie's withdrawing in order to write her poetry which ultimately drew us closer together.

She had always struck me as being in search of something; but I never knew what it was. I don't suppose that she knew, either — forces within us which drive us are often faceless, I know — but it didn't make things any easier for either of us. We were living at odds with each other: me, placid and content, having finally found what I had come many miles and braved many terrors to find; and Aurélie, feeling trapped and listless, still searching. I couldn't wholly comprehend her search, because I did not share that creativity, that compulsion to make something out of nothing: being out on the sea by day and safe at home at night was sufficient for me. But I did understand the ache for something unattainable; and I mourned for her.

Her finding the poetry changed all that. Finally, finally she had a way of sharing all the wildness, all the shining visions and grotesque images which haunted her mind — they had a way of getting out, rather than spinning around and around inside her brain. It was slow, but she started noticing things more — people, and their feelings.

We began spending more time together after that, as well. Times when Marie would be asked to keep Mimi at her house for the evening, and we would be alone. We would take long walks then, walks down to the cove where we had first met, years ago already; and we talked, not about ourselves as individuals, but about ourselves as a couple. We talked about what it meant to share one's life with someone else, and about how we could give to each other.

Sometimes we didn't talk at all, just held hands and walked on the sand, or up the steep path to the headland. We would stop, with the sea air all around us, the spray spitting up wetness, and we would hold each other. I think that I usually reached for her first; but it was she who would hug me tightly against her. And later, in the cottage, with the fire dwindling and Mimi's breathing slow and regular, we would undress together, and any other world, any other life, would then cease to exist.

And the things that we said. . . . I don't suppose that there is anything that one can say to the person one loves which is new. . . . I grew frustrated with words (just as Aurélie was discovering their power!); saying "I love you" had become too trite, too mechanical. How did one put all of these overwhelming feelings into words? Was it possible? I would be with her sometimes, watching her or talking with her or simply holding her, and there would suddenly be a wave — I cannot describe it any other way — of feelings washing over me: feelings of overpowering love, of aching satisfied yet still hungering, of need and want and tenderness. I could never have expressed that to her, so I said, "I love you," and hoped that she would understand. How finite we are, how bound by our modes of expression!

I don't think that Aurélie was oblivious to my sense of helplessness. She would hold me tightly — sometimes too tightly — and whisper fiercely, over and over again, "Philippa. Philippa," as though she, too, could not find the words to speak. I felt closest to her then, when she was not being self-assured or distant, when we were saying the same thing to each other in our silences.

And it was so *good* . . . good to be with her, to talk and laugh and make love, to whisper silly names to each other under our covers at night, to giggle as though we were of an age with Mimi, to go down to the beach and run and run until we fell exhausted on the sand, laughing and gasping for air. I'd fall onto my back and stare up at the sky, blue and crisp, white clouds dancing before the wind, and talk once my breath came back.

"I thank God every day for bringing me here. Remember the first day?"

She, too, was watching the sky. "How could I forget? I thought that you would die."

"Were you frightened?"

She turned on her side to look at me. "Of course not, Philippa. I had seen it all. I knew that you would be here."

I smiled. "Ah, but you didn't know then that I was your intended!"

And she would throw sand at me and scramble up, and I would chase her, and we were off again. But she had learned to laugh at some of her visions, and I had learned to take some of them more seriously, so I suppose that we were growing more together during those years.

Mimi was discovering her own path. It must have been difficult for her, knowing that the mist-laden fiery visions were in her blood, yet rooted as Aurélie never was in the life of the village. Her friends were all there, especially her closest friend, Adèle — Marie's daughter — and they would not have understood that side of her. I doubt whether she understood it herself; the gift did not, as Aurélie always reminded me, come at will — which I suppose was frightening. I saw things sometimes, too, but only with the aid of one of Aurélie's potions that her mother had taught to her: it was not in my veins. For Mimi it was, and it was an uneasy gift.

My sense was that it would not be such a bad thing to let it go altogether. Mimi had friends, a real life among people; she did not need to tread such a lonely path. With time, the visions would fade to half-remembered dreams, and Mimi would grow old with grandchildren around her knee rather than images in her head. It seemed a good idea.

Aurélie didn't think so. A gift, she insisted, is a gift, and must be developed. "We are not given to choose such things, Philippa. It is given or it is not given. Chantale did not pay attention to her dreams, and much good it did her! Her life was short and dull and grey — do you wish such a thing for Mimi?"

I was hurt. "I never had the visions, Aurélie, not as I grew up. But my life was good, it was full and exciting at times. If you have a stronger hold on reality, perhaps you don't require the other."

"You are different. To you it was not given, except through me. But Mimi — she is my mother's grandchild, she has the gift, and with it comes responsibility. If she does not own the images, then they will come to own her."

I argued in vain, for she was adamant. She didn't take Mimi straight up to the standing stones, and I credited her for that — it would have been too easy. But they sat and talked the dream-language which was so foreign to me, and I went down to the church in the village and knelt and wondered to God and all the saints if there was not some danger in all of this. It was too magical for me; I feared it. Perhaps I never really understood it.

Aurélie did find, though, that Mimi's gifts were not her

own. Mimi never went to the standing stones as Aurélie did:
she did not hear the voices, and was content to see visions in
the firelight. I think that Aurélie may have been disappointed
by this; in many ways, she thought of Mimi as her daughter —
we both did, by then — and wanted to give her all the good
things of her own life; but Mimi was another person. Aurélie
never really understood that she could not recapture her
mother in Mimi.

I was glad that the menhirs held no attraction for Mimi. I
had been to them once myself, going up without telling
Aurélie, feeling only the mists sinking damp and cold and
clammy through my shirt, and with them the cold hand of
fear. The stones were tall, majestic — yet I felt no comfort, no
sense of protection from them, only the eerie feeling that
there was somebody, somewhere, watching me. I am not
ashamed to admit that I began to run as soon as I had emerged
from the trees and I was on the path.

Aurélie knew, of course. She knew as soon as I walked
into the cottage, and she was angry. I tried to tell her that I had
gone so that I could understand that part of her, but she dismissed that summarily.

"You do not belong there. You should have known not to
go."

"You have never walked into a church to see what it was
like? You never wonder about that part of my life?"

"It is yours, Philippa. And the stones are mine. There is
power there — power to harm as well as to heal. You must
never, never go again. Please tell me that you will never go
again. I would fear too much for you."

She meant it, I knew that; and I gave in. I wasn't particularly drawn to the stones; I had simply wanted to go from
sheer curiosity.

But it told me something else about Aurélie, as well.
Before, had I gone, she would have been enraged because of
her need for privacy and solitude; now she objected out of fear

for me. And, in some way, I was gratified: Aurélie did not easily express feelings of caring, and I knew that that was precisely what she was doing. I never went again.

I knew that Aurélie cared for me, although I didn't really
understand how. For me, all love had to be rooted in faith —
which, obviously, was the Christian faith — for I deeply believed that God was love, and that all love flowed from God,
was given as a gift from Him. I felt close to Aurélie when I was
kneeling in the church in prayer, when I received the Sacra-
ments, when I sang the responses at Mass. It was difficult for
me to understand that love could come from different places,
that she could love me without loving (or even acknowledg-
ing) my God.

I was glad that we had no such conflict over Mimi. She
learned about her visions from Aurélie, and sometimes could
tell us of vivid dreams which she alone understood; but she
went to Mass with me on Sundays and prayed the rosary every
Friday with the rest of her class. Many of her subjects at
school were being taught at that time by the village priest,
especially history and religion, and I saw her as being interested and involved in her faith. Aurélie and I were two polari-
ties: Aurélie, pagan, totally rejecting the notion of organized
religion; and me, Catholic, immersed in my faith. But Mimi
was neither; she took what she needed from each: from the visions and the voices, from the Eucharist and the prayers.
Somehow, I envied her: she seemed more of a whole person
because of it than were either Aurélie or myself.

We had finally told her.

It was terribly difficult to do. We — Aurélie and myself —
were by that time so secure in ourselves, in our love and our
life together, that it was difficult to explain something which
to us required no explanation. But for Mimi it would, and we
spent long evenings talking together, trying to decide how
best to tell her. Aurélie, in her new-found compassion, was

suddenly gentler than me; she spoke of love and attraction, while I emphasized the need for silence. We finally walked out to the cove one Sunday afternoon, the three of us, Mimi with her kite, and we flew the kite and ate a picnic lunch — I can still taste it: crisp fresh bread, and cheese just soft, and red wine and sweet peaches. And at length we sat on the sand and talked together, and we told her.

She already knew.

Perhaps it had been in a vision — she didn't tell us much about her visions. Perhaps she had seen it all already: my flight to Saint-Malo and the convent, the first night that we spent together, Aurélie carefully cutting my hair short. Perhaps it was merely intuition — Mimi had always been a sensitive child. But she knew, and smiled at our anxiety.

"Haven't you noticed how I have never called you Papa?"

"I know. I thought—"

"Well, that's why. I knew already. But it's all right. You love each other, and I love both of you, and doesn't that make us a family?"

Aurélie reached out and hugged Mimi. "Of course it does. We'll always be a family."

I still had some concerns. "Mimi, you must understand that people in the village—"

She knew that, too. "They would not understand either, I know. It is really all right; I know what they can hear and what they cannot."

I felt better after that day, as though some cloud which had been following me about had suddenly vanished. Nothing seemed to have changed; but that which I had been dreading for years had been taken care of; and I was content.

There was, though, one change. From that day, Mimi stopped playing with names. After that, she called me Philippa, and Aurélie, Aurélie. In public, she called us nothing at all.

## XXIII 1868

# Aurélie:

*I* felt, sometimes, as one who had come from a wild country and had at last found shelter in a mountain hut. Or, to put it in terms that Philippa could understand, that I had been tossed about on a stormy sea and had finally found a safe harbor.

All of my dreams had been leading me places without my controlling them. Yet, the more that I wrote, the more that I explored my relationship with Philippa and with Mimi, the more I felt as though I could use the visions to speak to me, rather than as an end in and of themselves. It was a great feeling of power.

I still went to the standing stones, of course. I went, and saw the visions, shining and glowing and golden; I went, and heard the voices, haunting and beckoning and caressing; but I could leave them, too, and go back to the cottage on the headland. I was neither a witch nor a wife, but had found my path between them; and I was happy with it.

Marie sensed none of my struggle. With the men — and Philippa — out on the boats, going after the fish, Marie would talk with me about domestic concerns, and I would listen to her and wonder at how much emptiness was inside her head. She calmly took for granted that my interests were the same as hers, that nothing counted for me but my family and my house and my cooking. We walked the headland path, as did all the women of Saint Pol, particularly when the water was rough or the weather was bad, and the wind would catch at our skirts, and I would thrill to its wild touch — and Marie would be talking about soups. She annoyed me less than she had in the old days, for I felt sorry for her — her world was so less rich than mine. And yet sometimes I couldn't help but wonder how a strong grown woman could be so silly.

And then we would catch sight of the little fishing fleet, still far off, specks on the horizon, and she would speak of nothing but the men. They would be cold, and hungry, and tired; what would I prepare for my Philippe to eat when he got in? If there was sun that day, it would be reflecting off the water of the harbor, glittering golden in the late afternoon, dazzling and blindingly bright. And the boats would enter the brightness, and we would go down the path from the headland — not the small one which led down to the cove, no one from the village went there with any frequency — but the other, the path leading to the harbor. Marie would be laughing and bubbling, and I would sometimes feel some affection for her then — she was so happy.

And so we went down to the harbor, and she would run to her husband, and forget about me. I never ran to greet Philippa: it was not in me. I would wait until she was quite finished unloading, and then she would look around and see me waiting, and we would smile to each other, but still I did not run to her. I wondered sometimes whether my mother had ever run to greet my father, in the early days, when we still lived in the village and people still thought of my mother as being normal. I rather thought not.

So I would wait, and at length she would join me, and we would walk back up the headland path to the cottage.

Marie still saw something in me that was different — she chided me, for example, about not going to church, and wondered aloud that my husband did not insist that I go; but, by and large, it was as though the early years were a stage I had grown out of, a murky past that was best left forgotten. I went to her house in the village sometimes, and we sat and drank strong tea and talked of our children, and sometimes other women from the village would be there as well — women I had known in school, but had seen little of in the ensuing years — and we all were as one. Sometimes I could hear the voices in the back of my head, and I knew that I should be up on the headland; but I now sensed in myself the power to choose whether or not to respond to the call. Sometimes I excused myself and left; and sometimes, now, I stayed and talked until the time came to watch for the boats. It was part of my claiming time, when I claimed my individuality, my life, my relationship with Philippa, and my own needs: and it was a good time for me.

So Philippa and I would walk back up the path to the headland, sometimes with our arms around each other, sometimes holding hands, and she was tired and smelled of fish, and I would laugh at her and we would play games, me refusing to kiss her until she had bathed. She always bathed: Philippa never lost that convent training which required absolute cleanliness.

And the night would fall, and Mimi would study her lessons in the firelight, and I would sometimes read some of my poetry to Philippa, or she would read one of her mail-order books while I cleaned up the dishes from supper. And, at length, Mimi would go to bed, and we would be alone. I liked

those intimate quiet moments best, when the day was over
and everything behind us. Philippa always wanted to talk, to
speak words of love to me; but I was content with the silence.
I had always lived in silences; they held no fear for me. I
would trace the outline of her profile with my finger, and lean
over her and kiss her, my hair trailing all about us. And we
would hold each other in the firelight, and sometimes it
would be passionate, and sometimes it would be filled with
tenderness, but the love was always there, spun strong and
golden between us, holding us and linking us, even when we
were far from each other. It was always good, that time.

Learning and growing with another person had become
important to me. The times by the fire, the walks on the sand,
the dinners (which we avoided, but laughed over later) at
Marie's house in the village, the talks and the laughter and the
tears, the anger and the sorrow and the joy — it was all important to me, far more important than my mist-laden solitudes
and my echoing voices. I had learned what it was that they
were echoing, those voices and visions: they were echoing the
reality that I had found with Philippa.

I suppose, in a way, one could call that growing up. For
nearly twelve years, Philippa and I grew up together.

What else can I say about those years? That we never quar-
relled, Philippa and I? That would be nonsense: of course we
did, long screaming sessions after which she would retreat to
the church or the harbor, and I would go to the standing stones
— we each had our comfort. But the arguments brought us
closer, always: I sometimes understood Philippa better
through them then I did through the visions. I saw her passions, her rages, the things that she cared fiercely about, in a
way that was never revealed to me by the menhirs. And the
passions made us more part of each other, because they
touched off common chords in each of us. The visions told me
what she did: the rages told me who she was.

And peace, at last, would always follow.

Shall I say, then, that we were always happy? We were not. The days of depression came to both of us, sometimes as individuals, sometimes together: the greyness that is in the soul, even when the skies are a brilliant blue.

There was a sadness that we had imposed silence on Mimi, that she had to carry a secret with her, daily, when she went down to the village. It couldn't be helped, of course: but that didn't mean that we liked it. And there was sadness, too, for ourselves — how many times did I bite my tongue, when talking with Marie, to stop myself from stumbling over a pronoun? Too many times to count. And Philippa spoke to me once, in a voice filled with loneliness and longing, of confessions filled with lies, for she could not tell the priest the truth. It was a sadness that we carried with us, always; and yet, in a strange way, it too bound the three of us together even more closely.

Other things, too, disturbed our lives. Sometimes the catch was bad and food was scarce; one winter we lived almost entirely on the vegetables I had stored from the previous summer, and more than once we went to bed with hunger rumbling in our stomachs. Sometimes there was loneliness, when the winds kept the trawler out on the ocean for days on end, while Marie and I paced the headland and waited and waited. But these were the things we were used to: life is never what we want it to be, only what we can make of it. The god who speaks from the standing stones does not always give visions of happiness: but they are visions of life, and that is all that we need.

Until the day that the sky was clear and the sea was calm and the boat was late.

Marie and I were on the headland path, laughing about the large catch that had kept the boat out of the harbor, not worried — tragedies belong to storms and high winds, not to glass-like seas and gentle clouds. We talked and laughed and

joked together, walking the old path made smooth by generations of women before us, by our own mothers, talking of fish
and children and ordinary things. I remember — we were talking about Mimi's birthday, which was quickly approaching: I
could scarcely believe that she was going to be fifteen years
old. We had bought a bottle of the finest wine that Saint Pol
could boast of, and Philippa had found a book that Mimi was
sure to love. Marie was laughing and teasing me:

"You must be feeling old, with her fifteen!"

"You should talk: we're the same age, you and I. Don't
speak before you look for the grey in your own hair."

"Aurélie! What an awful thing to say!"

We walked and waited until the sky darkened and the
black clouds rolled in from the west and the wind picked up.
There was to be a storm, after all. We went back to my house
— Mimi was still down in the village at a piano lesson — and
sat drinking tea, Marie covering her anxiety with still more
talk.

"Well, with the wind picking up, they've probably gone
into another harbor down the coast. Don't you think so,
Aurélie? It would be far more sensible, after all...."

I couldn't respond. Times of stress, for me, have never
been times to be sociable. I sat, sipping the scalding hot tea
and listening to the rain which had come in off the sea: a light
patter at first, then gaining strength, whipping the trees and
the cottage door. Marie might have convinced herself that
they were safe; but I knew better. This time, there was no vision, no voice of doom, no prophetic image: but I knew.

It was dark night before they came up from the village.

The priest was there, as usual — Catholics seem to be so
overly concerned with other people's affairs, as if only they
hold the key to comfort. There were others, as well: the doctor, and Marie's brother Lucien, and one or two others. I don't
know how long they had waited before venturing up the path:

it was not the rain and the wind which kept them from coming. Even after so many years, everyone in the village still believed that a witch walked the headland path, still believed that my mother's curse lay heavy on the house.

As, in a way, it did.

Marie jumped up as soon as the door opened, crying out something unintelligible: then she saw their faces in the lamplight, and she knew. They came in silently, crowding into the little room; and part of my mind noticed that Mimi wasn't with them, they had carefully kept her down in the village out of harm's way, just as so many years ago Marie had taken her baby with her when I came to tell her of my mother's death.

We all stayed there for moment in silence, frozen in the lamplight into a tableau that defied time to continue. I stayed where I was, sitting at the table, my elbows leaning on it for support. There was no fire in the fireplace, but the newcomers all clustered around it anyway, its dead black ashes offering an imagined warmth, as though the life which once was there might somehow be revived by hope. Marie stood stiffly, staring at them in silence, her knuckles white as she gripped the back of the chair.

It was Lucien who spoke at length, stiffly, looking only at Marie; but he had come for her, after all. "Yves Laroue was over from Saint-Catherine. The banks have been rich there, this season... he said that the trawler was there today."

Marie let go of the chair, then, and gripped her brother's arm. "So they're all right! They put in to Saint-Catherine! It's all right, after—"

He cut her off with a voice steady as a monotone. "The trawler burned off their banks. No one knows how the fire started. They were pretty far out and most of Saint-Catherine's fleet was out beyond the point themselves, with no way of getting word to them. They sent what they had out, anyway, but they were too late. They couldn't even find anybody in the water." He pulled her closer to him, then, in a protective gesture. "I'm sorry, Marie. There were no survivors."

No. There were survivors.

I had tried to live without Philippa once. Images flooded in — not of Philippa alive and vibrant and smiling, but of the days and weeks and months that I had spent without her, when she had run away to Saint Malo and I hadn't the courage to ask her to stay. The images were clear and sharp: the misty melancholy, the long empty silences, the flatness and tiresomeness of everyday events, without her to enliven them. And the visions. . . .

The visions were all of darkness and death, of unspeakable terrors and unimaginable wildness. There was fear and blackness and emptiness when Philippa left, and it was only Mimi's need for me that kept me sane.

Mimi didn't need me any more, and the darkness hovered about me in the cottage on the headland, waiting, encroaching upon me, while the rain and the wind pounded and screamed outdoors.

I had been able to live without Philippa once. I knew, with all of myself, that I would not be able to do it again.

Marie was sobbing, and clutching at Lucien as if her hold on him could maintain her hold on reality as well. No one in the room seemed distressed by her tears: that is how we mourn, in Saint Pol — grief is neither quiet nor private when it is an expected part of one's life. Why, then, was I unable to formulate any words, unable even to cry? Was my way so very different from the way of my people?

I sat numbly listening to her for a few minutes more, listening also to the priest who had sat down next to me and was saying things that I didn't understand, and then I stood up from the table and walked outside.

The rain lashed at me like a whip, stinging and painful.

For a moment, before I closed the door, the lights spilled over the threshold, promising warmth and dryness and company: but it was the cold outside, the rain and wind and darkness with its terrible secrets, which had taken Philippa from me; and it was there that I needed to be. Behind me, in the house, someone was saying, "Let her go. She's always liked to be alone. It will help her."

I never said good-bye to Mimi. I might have done, had I been a better parent to her — but Philippa had been the better parent, and even she had left without a farewell. I walked up the path to the cliff and looked out at the darkness, sensing rather than seeing the black water below, the wind shrieking grief around me and the rain streaking down my collar and through my hair. The water below hissed and swirled, the water which had brought her to me and had taken her away from me.

And then I jumped.

# Epilogue

# Mimi:

The government was looking for a place to spend some money. I don't suppose that they ever considered buying food for those who are hungry... the government in Paris isn't very sensible, sometimes. What they wanted to make was a sort of *beau geste*, do something noticeable; and, for some reason, they chose Brittany.

A literary type was sent to wander up and down the coast — a foreigner, he was, from Paris — and he talked to the people who would talk to him (many of us merely shrugged and claimed that we didn't speak French, we only spoke Breton: no one really likes foreigners). He asked them about stories of their villages, and legends, and he wrote everything down in a small notebook that he carried around with him. He seemed fascinated by the most ordinary things: the fishing, and the cold, and the hardships and the waiting.

He was quite taken by it all; but he was especially interested when he came to Saint-Pol-des-Fougères and he heard the story of the woman who had killed herself in grief when her husband had failed to come home from the sea. It was a tragedy, people told him; but he remained interested nonetheless.

He wrote about it, I think, in a book; and people read about it. And one day some people came from Paris and spoke with the mayor and the doctor and the priest, and then they built a statue up on the headland. It represented a man dressed in fishing gear, with his arm around a woman's shoulders; she had a shawl pulled tightly about her, and her eyes saw only the waves out beyond.

There were speeches, and applause, and everyone was smiling and talking together. It was supposed to be for all of the fishermen of Brittany, and for all of their widows; but they put it in Saint Pol for the fisherman who had died and for the woman who killed herself rather than live without him.

I didn't know what to think. Adèle had come to live with me on the headland by that time — we had long since accepted the miracle of our friendship shifting into love — and we talked about it together. Sometimes I just wanted to forget them: their deaths were still painful for me to think of; but part of me rejoiced to see the people I had loved for so long honored in such public way.

Their names were inscribed on the pedestal of the statue; and I walked up there sometimes. I would sit there on the ground; leaning against the statue, dreaming and listening to the past.

Marie and all the others were pleased about the statue, even though no one would admit it: too many foreigners had come already, and others came to look at it, and watch the fishermen coming in at night. They were pleased that Adèle had come to live with me: she would help me through my grief, help me get a fresh start on life. We had hated the distance between us: we realized, quite naturally, that we preferred each other's company to that of anyone else, and that we wanted to be together, always. We wrote each other notes, sometimes, exchanging them surreptitiously at Mass or in the marketplace; but we were relieved when we didn't have to do it anymore. There was no question of pretending that one of us was a man: we simply had to pretend that our friendship was in fact no more than that. No one thought anything of it — why should they have done?

And Adèle and I lived happily in the house on the headland, for almost two decades; and no one minded. We had good times, and bad times; I sometimes went up to the standing stones, but Adèle never showed any interest. She liked my poetry, and encouraged me: it was because of her persistence that I sent out a few of them to Paris, to a publisher who wrote back sending me money and asking for more. Adèle was all for us moving to the city on the spot, where I could be closer to my work, and we could live anonymously; but I could never leave the cliffs, and the menhirs, and all that gave me life.

But the poems became books, and we were able to live quite comfortably on what I earned from them. Adèle bought a fine large loom, and spent most of her time weaving — not just for us, but beautiful tapestries that she sent off to Saint Malo and Epernay and Paris; a writer even came one spring to interview her.

And then a winter came when Adèle couldn't move from bed. The doctor came up to the house on the headlands again and again; but the fever persisted, and on the fourth day Adèle died. Marie and I stood side by side at her funeral, clinging to each other, crying and mourning together.

Spring came slowly that year, and in its dreary beginnings Marie cleared out Adèle's old room in her house. I didn't know that there was a box in that room containing all of the notes I had written to Adèle while she still lived in the village, letters of love and encouragement and hope, letters which told her of Aurélie and Philippa, tied up in a frayed velvet ribbon. I didn't know that Marie sat in the fading light reading all the notes, all the words of love that I had given to her daughter.

Marie had lost too much. Husband, daughter... and Aurélie had been her friend. She had no understanding of what had happened: she saw only the betrayal, the silences that Aurélie had left between them. And she began to hate.

She started the gossip in the village; she spoke of evil things... and she raised their voices against Philippa and Aurélie, until they brought their instruments of destruction and toppled the statue off into the sea.

It is over now. All of it. They will forget, in time; Marie will die one day, and other joys and sorrows will close in and take over other people's lives, and our story will grow old. That is how it always happens, in Breton villages like Saint Pol.

And I will be alone.

It is not such a terrible thing, being alone. I will continue to go up to the standing stones, as Aurélie knew that I would; and the voices and visions will lull me and seduce me, until the village and the hatred and the pain will no longer matter to me. The images of the ripped portrait and the destroyed statue will fade in my heart; and the people will come to speak of me as they came to speak of my grandmother Iseut: the insane one, the witch. And I will no longer care.

We are leaving behind a legend, all of us: because we have lived here, others will know that it has been done — others will dare to love and trust and feel as we did. For that I am grateful: and it will have to be enough, for it is all that I have.

And the world will go on. *Plus ça change, plus c'est la même chose.*